Isabella Vasquez

WANTED:
DEAD OR ALIVE

WILLIAM GALE

For Shari, my patient and encouraging wife, whose suggestion
inspired me to write Bella's backstory.

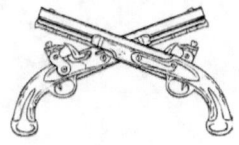

INTRODUCTION

Isabella Vasquez is a secondary character in two of my previous novels: *A Pirate's Daughter* and *Captain Skelly O'Keeffe; Around the Horn*. Some readers have found Bella to be one of the more intriguing characters in those books. Her background story was sketchy. Born a rich girl, how was it she ended up as a member of a pirate crew on Red Ned O'Keeffe's ship, the *Queen Maeve*? So Dear Reader, what follows is the tale of how she fled a comfortable life of privilege on her father's hacienda, and through circumstances beyond her control, turned to a life of outlawry, and eventually piracy. This is Bella's story.

Part One

HACIENDA BELLE

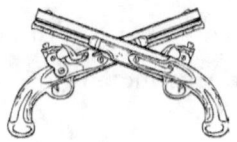

CHAPTER ONE

It was late in the evening on the first day of June 1765, and Ana Maria Navarro Vasquez let out yet another bloodcurdling scream. She lay in bed, exhausted, drenched in sweat, her jet-black hair plastered to her head in limp ringlets. She had been in labor for twelve hours. The midwife urged her, "Now, Señora one more push. I see baby's head." Ana, with the aid of a native Indian serving girl, Sesasi, raised her head and shoulders and pushed with all of her remaining strength. Spent, she fell back onto the pillow. Sesasi mopped Ana's damp forehead with a soft towel. The room fell silent for a moment, and then the quiet was broken by the wail of a newborn infant.

"Señora Vasquez, you have a beautiful baby daughter," the midwife said, as she tied off the infant's umbilical cord with a piece of red yarn. She wrapped the newborn in a clean cloth and gently laid the baby on her mother's breast.

The ordeal over, Ana was revived by the cry of her newborn child. She cuddled the infant, marveling at the baby girl's furrowed brow, her perfect little fingers, the minuscule finger nails, the surprisingly thick head of black hair covering the infant's head. She turned to Sesasi and said, "Tell the Don he has a daughter." The Indian girl nodded and left the room.

Taking refuge in the library of Casa Del Rio Verde, Don Domingo Vasquez, sitting at his ornately carved desk, fidgeted anxiously with a slender dagger he used as a letter opener. He had come up with a grand name for his hacienda despite the fact that there was no river, green or otherwise, near the property. He sipped tawny, ten-year-old Spanish port from a silver cup as the cries of his young wife echoed throughout the house. Her screams had been going on for an interminably long time, unnerving the Don. In his years serving in the army, he had seldom been afraid, regardless the peril, but listening to the pain-filled cries of his beautiful young wife was unsettling, as well as somewhat annoying.

Domingo Vasquez was a Creole, that is he was of pure Spanish blood, but had been born in Mexico, thereby relegating him to a form of second-class citizenship. All high offices in politics, in the Church, and in the militarily were reserved for Spaniards born in Iberia. When the Mexican national army was created to protect Spain's sovereignty in Mexico, it provided an avenue for men like Domingo Vasquez to rise in society.

He left his parents' modest farm at the age of eighteen and joined the army. He was smart, ambitious, and exhibited an extraordinary degree of bravery and resourcefulness, which saw him elevated to the rank of Lieutenant in only two years, leapfrogging non-commissioned officer ranks. He served with distinction for several years as a lieutenant, was promoted to Captain, and was given the command of a company of men in the South of Mexico. Because he was not Iberian born, however, captain was the highest rank attainable for one such as Domingo Vasquez.

By serving in a remote post Domingo found there was ample opportunity for an ambitious young man to supplement his meager military wages. Often landowners needed protection from bandits and were willing to pay. On occasion miners wishing to explore areas under the control of the army paid for the privilege of excavating on otherwise off-limit lands. Fortune seekers, such as those wishing to cultivate vineyards, or to plant olive trees in remote locations away from the prying eyes of government officials paid handsomely for Captain Domingo Vasquez to look the other way. The government in Spain forbade the growing of grapes and olives in Mexico because vintners and olive growers in Spain feared the competition and wanted to protect their lucrative trade agreements. Mexico was a Spanish colony, and everything that was done in Mexico was done solely for the benefit of the Spanish Crown.

After serving in the army as a captain for ten years, Domingo Vasquez had accumulated a small fortune. He lived modestly on his captain's salary and the extra money he acquired had been stashed away for the future in banks in Mexico City. Domingo had big plans. He had seen lavish haciendas, land grants to Spaniards loyal to the crown, and he wanted that lifestyle for himself.

He left the army at the age of thirty-four, bought a parcel of land two hours north of the capital, Mexico City, and began purchasing horses and cattle. He hired several Mestizos, half Spanish-half Indian ranch hands to help manage the herds. His intention was to expand his holdings with an eye to selling horses and cattle to the military. The army was always in need of horses for mounted troops and cattle to feed hungry soldiers.

Domingo Vasquez obtained a small contract to furnish horses and cattle to a local regiment. It was a profitable venture, and he plowed the proceeds into buying more land and more livestock. He hired an Indian woman to serve as cook and housekeeper. He took on several more Mestizos to tend the herds, and he began construction on a new casa, much grander than the small adobe abode that had come with the property. His

hacienda had grown considerably, his herds had increased, and he nego-
tiated a larger and more favorable contract with the General in charge of
the Central District. He had a reputation for being able to deliver superb,
healthy horses of pure Spanish descent in a timely manner, and his beef
cattle were prized by both the army and butchers in the capital city.

Hard work had paid off handsomely for Domingo Vasquez, and he
was conferred the title of Don, despite the fact that he was Mexican born.
He had become a wealthy man, and wealth was influence. He liked to
throw lavish dinners for members of the colonial government and the
military at his spacious new home. Feting dignitaries on prime beef and
expensive wines imported from Spain brought him recognition and even
more lucrative contracts.

From humble beginnings as a farmer's son, to becoming one of the
wealthiest men outside of Mexico City, Don Vasquez' rise in social status
was the fulfillment of his dreams. Unable to attain a high ranking military position of his own, he now was courted by generals and politicians.
The only thing missing from his life was an heir. At the age of forty-six,
Don Vasquez began looking for a suitable wife.

The Don was quite particular regarding the qualities he desired in a
mate. He wanted a woman young enough to bear a number of children.
She had to come from a good family, preferably one of pure Iberian descent. She must be attractive, both physically, and in her demeanor, and
it would be a plus if her father was socially prominent. He let it be known
that he was interested in marriage, and soon a number of important fig-
ures invited Don Vasquez to their homes to meet unwed daughters, or
brought their daughters to Casa Del Rio Verde for the frequent dinners
the Don hosted. At one such event a young woman of nineteen, Ana
Maria Navarro, youngest daughter of Philip Navarro, Assistant Viceroy
of the Colony of Mexico, caught the attention of the Don.

Ana Maria Navarro was a lovely, vibrant young woman. Her heart-
shaped face was framed by long, jet-black hair. Her intelligent eyes were

dark and lively. Born in Spain, she had remained there in the home of an uncle to complete her education when her father was appointed to the position of Assistant Viceroy in Colonial Mexico. Ana's mother had died when Ana was ten. Her older brother traveled with their father to Mexico, and Ana joined the family there when she turned eighteen.

Her father and brother, Miguel, lived in a palatial house in Mexico City. The two men lived a bachelor lifestyle. Miguel, like his father, worked in a government office, and was charged with overseeing agricultural affairs. When Ana arrived, she brought a breath of fresh femininity into the home.

Ana immediately took on the responsibility of overseeing the running of the Navarro household. Lazy servants were discharged, and she hired an experienced cook to make sure wholesome, hearty meals were waiting for her father and brother when they arrived home, tired and hungry from long days working in their government offices.

Philip Navarro had big plans for his daughter. It was well known that Don Domingo Vasquez was looking for a wife, and the Don was a very wealthy man. The fact that Don Vasquez was a Creole could be overlooked given the extent of the man's vast holdings in land and herds. Philip visited Casa Del Rio Verde, ostensibly to negotiate the purchase of horses for the various departments he oversaw. He took Ana along to "show her the countryside," knowing they would be invited to remain for dinner.

Philip's ploy worked. The minute Don Vasquez set eyes on Ana Navarro, he knew she was the one. Not only was she beautiful, but she was Iberian born, and her father held the second highest position in the colonial government. The Don knew his social standing would soar with Ana Navarro as his wife.

As for Ana, she was immediately attracted to the tall, dashing, self-confident master of Casa Del Rio Verde. Don Vasquez carried himself with an air of understated power derived from commanding a company of soldiers and the years of hard work that had brought him such great wealth. Ana thought Don Vasquez handsome, tall and slim, with a dapper moustache, and streaks of gray at his temples. His eyes were dark and penetrating. It bothered her not in the least that the Don was more than twice her age, nearly as old as her father. Two months later they were wed in the Cathedral of the Assumption of the Blessed Virgin Mary in Mexico City. Three months after the wedding, Ana was with child. Don Vasquez lit candles at the Cathedral and prayed to the Virgin that the child his wife carried would be a son.

Sesasi, the Indian servant girl, stood quietly for a long time outside the closed doors of the library, hesitatant to disturb Don Vasquez. Everyone on the hacienda was aware that the Master of the house had been hoping and praying for a son. Finally, she overcame her temerity and knocked softly on the thick, wooden door.

"Yes? Enter," Don Vasquez called out.

Sesasi, with eyes lowered and head bowed, opened the door and padded in bare feet into the room. "Señor, the baby is born. You have a beautiful daughter."

"A daughter?" The Don could not keep the disappointment out of his voice. With a slight nod of his head and casual wave of his hand, he dismissed the serving girl. Sesasi quickly backed out of the room and closed the door behind her.

Inside, Don Vasquez stabbed the dagger he had been playing with down hard, burying its needle-sharp point into the top of the desk. He muttered, "Damn!" and poured another cup of port.

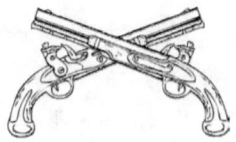

CHAPTER TWO

Late that night Don Vasquez ascended to his wife's bedroom. She was sleeping, as was the infant in the cradle beside the bed. In the light of the candle burning on the nightstand, the Don looked down on the baby girl, peaceful in repose. Such a tiny thing. An embroidered coverlet hid all but the child's face. The next one will be a boy, he told himself, and retired to his own rooms adjacent to his wife's.

The Don was awakened in the wee hours of the morning by the incessant bawling of the infant in the room next door. He was annoyed, and even after the crying ceased, found it impossible to fall back asleep. He had no experience with babies and no desire to learn. He rose, dressed, and went down to his sanctuary, the library.

Many books filled the shelves on the north wall of the library, but the Don had not read any of them. They were purchased in Mexico City merely for show. He had no desire to read anything that did not relate to his business interests. The Indian cook brought the Don's morning coffee to the library, and after smoking one of the long, slender cigars he favored, he went down to the stables. The sun was just coming up as he mounted one of his prized stallions and rode out to inspect his herds.

Ana awoke to the wailing of the baby girl who had been sleeping peacefully in her cradle at the bedside. Sesasi, also awakened by the infant's crying, rose from the blanket where she had been sleeping on the floor outside her mistress' door.

"Señora, she is hungry," Sesasi said, lifting the baby out of the cradle and placing her on her mother's breast. The baby ceased bawling and gurgled contentedly as she began to suckle.

"Señora, what will you name her?" Sesasi asked.

"I must consult with the Don, of course, but I want to name her Isabella Guadalupe. We can call her Bella."

"That is a beautiful name. She is a beautiful baby. She will grow up to be beautiful like her mother." Sesasi was a shy girl of eighteen, with big brown eyes, olive skin, and black hair worn in a long braid. At the age of twelve she had been "sold" to Don Vasquez by a business associate in Mexico City to serve in the household, cleaning and helping with kitchen chores. She had been forcibly converted to Catholicism shortly before being placed in service to the Don.

"When will she be baptized?" Sesasi asked, watching the baby feed.

"At two weeks," Ana replied. Ana was fond of Sesasi and had decided she wanted the Indian girl to help care for the baby. "We will have to travel to the city for the sacrament. Perhaps you would like to go with us to help." Don Vasquez had begun building a chapel adjacent to the casa, but it was not yet completed. It was a two hour drive by carriage to Mexico City, making it somewhat of a burden to attend Sunday Mass. It was the Don's intention to obtain the services of a friar to say Mass at the hacienda to avoid the weekly trips to the Cathedral.

Don Vasquez shrugged his shoulders. "Name her as you please," he said, standing at his wife's bedside. Ana was sitting up in the bed, propped by several pillows. She was feeding the baby who seemed to have an endless appetite. The Don had briefly held his infant daughter and was almost won over when the baby grasped his finger in her tiny hand. But then the baby began to bawl, and her father quickly passed the wailing infant to her mother.

"Who shall we ask to be her Godparent?" Ana asked.

"Your brother Miguel?"

"I will write to him. I am sure he would be honored."

Don Vasquez left the room, having had his fill of a crying baby.

Ana wondered if his attitude would have been different if the infant had been a boy.

Two weeks later, Ana Vasquez, holding baby Bella, and accompanied by Sesasi inside the carriage, made the trip to the Cathedral of the Assumption of the Blessed Virgin Mary. Don Vasquez rode alongside mounted on one of his prized horses. Two of his Mestizo hired hands, both armed with pistols and muskets, rode behind. Although the road to Mexico City was well-traveled, there was always the possibility of being waylaid by bandits. Don Vasquez carried a brace of pistols tucked into a broad sash tied around his waist, and his military rapier in its leather covered scabbard dangled from his left hip.

The party was met outside the Cathedral by Ana's father, Philip, and her brother, Miguel, who was delighted to have been chosen as his niece's Godparent. Sesasi and the two Mestizos remained outside in the cool shade of the Cathedral while the others entered the edifice through the heavily carved wooden doors. The Cathedral was nearly two-hundred-years-old and still not completed. Numerous architects had worked on it during that time, using a variety of building styles. Despite sometimes conflicting architectural touches, the Cathedral was, nevertheless, an impressive structure.

Inside the church Miguel tenderly cradled a sleeping, contented baby Bella, who had just finished feeding prior to arrival in the city. Bella was dressed in a white gown trimmed with fine Spanish lace, and it put Miguel in mind of holding his sister, Ana, when she was a newborn, and he a boy of ten. Now his baby sister was the mother of this beautiful child.

Because of Don Vasquez' status in society, the Bishop himself elected to perform the Baptism sacrament. Bishop Manuel Jose Rubio y Salinas had been sent from Spain to take on the duties of overseeing the Catholic Church in Mexico.

As the party gathered around the baptismal fount, the Bishop asked the parents, "What is the child's name?"

When Don Vasquez remained silent, Ana spoke up. "Her name is Isabella Guadalupe Vasquez, your Excellency."

"And who stands for this child?"

"I do, Excellency," Miguel Navarro replied.

"And what do you request of the Church?"

"Baptism, Excellency."

"On behalf of this child, do you renounce Satan and all of his works?"

"I do, Excellency."

The Bishop made the sign of the cross with his thumb on the baby's forehead, causing Bella to frown and wrinkle her brow, but her eyes remained closed.

Addressing Miguel, the Bishop asked, "Do you believe in God the Father, in Jesus Christ His Son, and in the Holy Spirit?"

"I do, Excellency," Miguel replied, answering on behalf of baby Bella. He held the baby's head over the baptismal fount.

The Bishop dipped a small gold cup into the water of the fount and blessed it. He dribbled a tiny stream of water over Bella's forehead three times, each time repeating, "Isabella, Guadalupe Vasquez, I baptize you in the name of the Father, the Son, and the Holy Spirit." As the water washed over her forehead, Bella squirmed, opened her eyes, made two tiny fists, and let out one small displeased cry. The Bishop completed the ceremony by dipping his thumb in oil and marking a cross on the baby's forehead. Baptism finished, the newly Christened Catholic was handed back to her mother, and the family repaired to Philip Navarro's house for a celebratory luncheon.

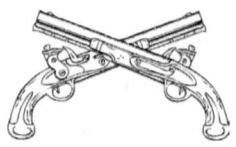

CHAPTER THREE

Father Fernando Diaz, a Dominican friar, arrived at Case Del Rio Verde on muleback. The padre's services had been obtained by Don Domingo Vasquez for the dual purpose of saying daily Mass in the chapel, which had finally been completed adjacent to the casa, and to serve as a tutor for four-year-old Isabella.

Bella, a precocious child, had already taken an interest in the books in her father's library. She liked to look at the ones with illustrations and occasionally added a few childish pictures of her own using a quill pen and ink. Don Vasquez was unaware of his daughter's doodles because he never opened any of the books. It was Bella's mother, Ana, who discovered her daughter's artistic efforts after finding the girls small fingers black with ink. Spanking Bella was futile; the little girl almost never cried, and generally scampered off laughing after receiving a swift swat on the rear.

The Don's intention of having a priest in residence to say Mass had finally come to fruition, but it was Ana's idea to bring in the padre to tutor the child. "She is ready to read," Ana insisted one evening, speaking to her husband at the dinner table. Don Vasquez was indifferent to his daughter's education. His hopes of having a son and heir had been dashed when, after four years, Ana had been unable to get pregnant again.

Father Diaz was an amiable man in his early fifties, somewhat rotund, his gray robes stretched taut across his ample belly. He was a scholar and came highly recommended for the position at Casa Del Rio Verde by the Bishopric in Mexico City. The position suited him well. His simple needs would be met, good food, good wine, his own small house adjoining the chapel, with plenty of time to pursue his studies. He was writing a history of the indigenous peoples of Mexico, a work that had occupied him for a number of years. Like Don Vasquez, Father Diaz was a Creole, of Spanish blood, but born in Mexico. He could never ascend to a higher clerical position than that of a simple parish priest despite having attended seminary in Spain. His duties at Casa Del Rio Verde seemed easy enough, say Mass every morning, and spend a few hours a day instructing the young daughter of one of the wealthiest men in Central Mexico. The rest of the time was his own to devote to research and writing.

Father Diaz arrived at the hacienda late in the day, after Bella had already been fed, bathed, and tucked into bed by Sesasi. One of the servants showed the padre to his quarters and stabled his mule. The cook brought the priest's dinner and a bottle of Spanish wine to his modest new home. Modest though the friar's house might be, it seemed the lap of luxury to him. It was furnished with a clean, comfortable bed, a table and chair for taking his meals, and a desk where he could carry on with his studies and writing. The food was delicious, a braised beef stew with plenty of meat and not just vegetables, a pleasant change from the simple fare to which he had been accustomed. The wine was superb. Yes, he thought, I will like this position very much.

In the morning, after saying Mass for an audience of one, Sesasi, Father Diaz met Bella. He was immediately taken with the child, as pretty and energetic a little girl as he had ever seen. Her inky black curls contrasted with her pale complexion. He saw intelligence in her big, dark eyes, but also a mischievous glint. Unbeknownst to the padre, Bella had a wild streak, an untamed impish disposition. She was forever playing childish tricks on the servants, especially Sesasi, whom she loved as much as she did her own mother. Bella's father, the Don, was the one person she never teased or tricked, and he would have been appalled at his daughter's behavior had he been aware of it. Too busy with his own affairs to notice Bella's rambunctious mischief, there was no one to rein in the girl. Bella's mother indulged her only child, allowing the girl to race around the house, climb on furniture, and generally do as she pleased. When it was time to corral the girl for dinner and bath, Bella was as likely to be found in the stables talking to the horses, or in the yard pestering the dogs, as she was playing with dolls in her bedroom.

Bella's mother introduced Bella to Father Diaz. "Father is going to teach you how to read and write. He will teach you mathematics, and history. It will be fun." Ana Vasquez showed the priest to a small room opposite the library equipped with a round table and two chairs. Paper, pens, and ink were neatly arranged on the tabletop.

"Well, I will leave you to it," Ana said, and left the room.

Bella planted her hands on her hips and stared defiantly at the priest. "I want to play."

"Yes, my child, and so you shall after your lessons are finished." Father Diaz leaned down close to the small girl, revealing the bald top of his head surrounded by a fringe of brown hair shot through with gray.

"Your head is bald in the middle."

"Yes, it is called a tonsure. It signifies I am a man of God. Now come child, sit, and we will begin your lessons. We shall start with Latin."

"What is Latin?"

"It is the language of the Bible. It is the language of the Mass."

"Why? The Mass should be in Spanish so everyone can understand."

"I see you are a bright child. You have an inquisitive mind. That is good, but do not ask too many questions. It is better to listen instead. Now, shall we begin? Let me give you an easy one to remember, *amo, amas, amat*. In Latin that means I love, you love, he, she, it loves."

Bella screwed up her face in a manner she had when something bothered her. "*It* means thing, and things cannot love. Only people can love. I love mama and Sesasi. I suppose I love Father, too, but I don't know if he loves me. Mommy tells me all the time she loves me, but Father never does."

"I'm quite sure your father loves you very much. He is a very busy man."

"Father wishes I was a boy." Bella reached out and grabbed one of the sheets of paper. Sliding it across the table so it was in front of her, she dipped one of the quill pens in the pot of ink and began to draw.

"Isabella, this is not the time for drawing pictures. Please, pay attention."

Bella ignored the priest and continued her drawing of a horse. "This is Diablo, father's horse."

The priest reached across the table and snatched the quill from Bella's hand. He grabbed the piece of paper, smearing the ink, and crumpled the childish drawing into a ball. Bella stared at him defiantly and reached for another piece of paper. Father Diaz slapped her hand. Bella let out a howl, more in anger than in pain. She slid off her chair and left the room.

A few minutes later Ana Vasquez appeared angrily in the doorway of the small room. "Father, you are never to strike my child again. Is that perfectly clear?"

The priest was taken aback. He was unaccustomed to being addressed in such a fashion, and especially not by a woman. He was at a loss for words.

Ana's expression softened a little. "I know Bella is a headstrong girl, Father, but she will come around. Be patient with her. She is a curious child, and I am certain you can find a way to reach her. She does not need to learn Latin at the age of four, but she is ready to learn to read and write. Start there." With that, Ana turned away. Bella did not return to the room. Apparently the lessons were over for the day.

Over the next several weeks Bella and Father Diaz achieved a detente of sorts. Latin was forgotten; the priest tried a different tactic, allowing the girl to ask questions, whatever came into her young head. He answered the easy ones on the spot, but more difficult inquiries provided the opportunity and impetus to encourage Bella to find the answers for herself. When she asked why the sun always came up in the east, for example, he led the girl into her father's library and found a volume on astronomy. He opened the book and read to her about the planets and stars, how the earth revolved around the sun, and because the earth constantly rotated in the same direction, the sun always appeared to rise in the east.

Discovering that the books in her father's library held more than illustrations, but also words that explained how things worked, was the push Bella needed to learn to read. Father Diaz taught her the alphabet, teaching her the sounds each letter made, and how the letters and their sounds could be combined to make words, and words could be joined together to make sentences.

By her fifth birthday Bella was reading with an amazing degree of proficiency, and was writing full, complex sentences. Father Diaz used the globe in the library to teach Bella geography, particularly where Spain was located at the southwestern corner of Europe, and Spain's many colonies in the New World, including Mexico. He used examples from around the rancho to introduce Bella to mathematics. How many chickens were there in the henhouse behind the casa? They spent part of an afternoon counting the hens. How many would be left if the cook took two pullets for Sunday dinner? If half of the chickens laid an egg on any given day, how many eggs could be collected to make breakfast or to use in baking Bella a cake?

Instead of confining Bella's studies to the small room, the entire casa and surrounding grounds became the classroom. Once their initial conflict was resolved, Bella became attached to her priestly tutor, and Father Diaz developed an unexpected fondness for his pupil. Bella began attending Mass in the chapel each morning with Sesasi, and immediately thereafter the day's lessons would begin. Hand-in-hand, the tall, heavyset priest and the slender, diminutive girl would explore the world around Casa Del Rio Verde, stopping to study a particular plant, or to watch swifts swooping and diving to catch insects on the wing.

Bella was a bright girl, learned quickly, and had an insatiable appetite for discovering the world around her. She would often scamper ahead, climb onto a fence or up into a tree to get a different view of things. Father Diaz sometimes had difficulty keeping up with his young charge, but there was always a smile on his face as he watched the girl romp fearlessly around the estate.

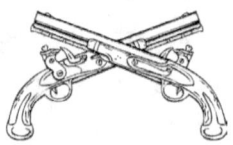

Chapter Four

"I want Father Diaz to do my First Communion," Bella said, frowning. She was seven, and after three years of studying daily with the priest had come to love the fat friar dearly. He was her teacher, but also her friend, practically her only friend other than Sesasi. There were no other children on the hacienda to play with. Bella's mother was constantly busy overseeing the household and the many dinners and parties held at Casa Del Rio Verde, and Bella's father, the Don, was cold and aloof, unapproachable. Father Diaz adored the child and was always there to answer her questions or listen to the little stories she liked to make up.

"Bella, dearest, the Archbishop will administer the sacrament at the Cathedral in the city," Ana explained patiently to her willful daughter. "Father Diaz may accompany us on the ride to the Cathedral, and perhaps the bishop will allow him to participate in saying the Mass. Hurry now, we must be on our way." Ana took Bella's hand and found it sticky. "Child, what have you been eating?"

"Mango," Bella replied.

"Holy Mother of God, look, you have a stain on your dress." Ana sighed in exasperation. "Run, wash your hands. We have to leave." Nothing could be done about the yellowish spot on the front of Bella's frilly and otherwise snow white First Communion dress.

Back from washing her hands, Bella climbed into the carriage where her mother, Sesasi, and Father Diaz were already seated and waiting. As was his custom, Don Vasquez was astride Diablo, his magnificent black stallion. As usual when making the trip to Mexico City, he was armed with his rapier and a brace of pistols. The two mounted Mestizo ranch hands who served as bodyguards were also armed, as was the servant driving the coach.

The party set out at a brisk pace. It was already after nine in the morning and the Mass was scheduled for eleven. It would not do to keep Archbishop Francisco Antonio de Lorenzano waiting. He had been sent from Spain to oversee the Church in Mexico when Bishop Salinas unexpectedly passed away, shortly after Bella's Baptism.

They arrived at the Cathedral with mere minutes to spare. Father Diaz quickly ushered Bella into the nave. A dozen other children, all dressed in white, the sons and daughters of prominent government officials, were already seated in the front row of pews, boys on the right and girls on the left. Immediately behind the row of girls, Bella's grandfather, Philip Navarro, and her uncle, Miguel, occupied the second pew, saving room for Don and Donna Vasquez. Father Diaz deposited Bella at the end of the row of girls and then took a seat farther back, behind the parents of the other children.

Bella turned in her seat and grinned at her grandfather and uncle, who was also her Godfather. "Hi, Poppa, hi Uncle," she said. She was fond of both men, even though she only saw them a few times a year. Her parents entered and sat next to Ana's father and brother. Don Vasquez had left his pistols and sword in the carriage under the watchful eyes of his hired hands. Sesasi crept into the church and took a seat in the very last row of pews.

Just then the Archbishop, flanked by two Franciscan priests and a cadre of altar boys carrying candles and incense burners, entered the sanctuary. Everyone in the nave stood as the Archbishop began the ritual of the High Mass. As the Mass progressed, Bella, unaccustomed to being still for long, squirmed in her seat as the Archbishop read the daily selection from the Gospels and the Epistles, and droned on and on spouting a sermon on the meaning and importance of Communion. Her mother laid a hand on Bella's shoulder and whispered harshly, "Be still, Child."

Finally it was time for the seven and eight-year-old children to receive their First Communion. They filed out of their pews, boys first, and lined up at the altar rail. As each child in turn knelt at the rail, the Archbishop lifted one of the communion wafers from the golden chalice and said, "The Body of Christ," as he laid the wafer on the child's extended tongue. A priest held a gold paten under each child's chin as the sacrament was administered lest the wafer fall and land on the floor. When it was Bella's turn she received the wafer and returned to her seat. Having been admonished by Father Diaz not to chew the wafer, she let it melt on her tongue. When she had asked him why she could not chew the wafer, he tried to explain that the wafer, a simple piece of unleavened bread, through the blessing of the priest was transformed into the actual body of Jesus. That made absolutely no sense to Bella. How could a piece of bread become a person? Still, she studiously avoided chewing the wafer because Father Diaz had told her it would be a grave sin to do so.

After the Mass, the Vasquez party went to Philip Navarro's residence for a luncheon in honor of Bella's First Communion. Her grandfather presented her with a rosary that had a solid gold cross and real ivory beads. Her Godfather, Uncle Miguel, gave her a velvet pouch containing seven gold Spanish doubloons, each one dated for one of her seven years.

Bella loaded a plate with treats from the lunch table and took it outside to Sesasi and the ranch hands. Father Diaz had been invited inside to dine with the family. It was late in the afternoon when the Vasquez family set out for home. Bella, tired and stuffed with delectable goodies, was sleeping, her head resting against Father Diaz' arm. Suddenly the carriage drew up sharply, and Bella was jolted awake.

"What is it? Are we home?" Bella asked, rubbing sleep from her eyes with her fists.

"No, I will see what the matter is," Father Diaz said, but before he could stir to exit the carriage, a gunshot rang out.

Thrusting aside the curtain covering the window, Don Vasquez peered into the carriage. "Robbers. Stay inside." He drew his pistols and put spurs to his horse's flanks. Diablo leapt forward and the Don fired one pistol and then a second. Bella jumped down from the seat and poked her head through the open window to see what was happening. More shots rang out, many more, and Bella saw one of the Casa Del Rio Verde ranch hands tumble from his horse.

Father Diaz grabbed Bella around the waist and pulled her back inside the carriage. Ana Vasquez had gone pale. Sesasi grabbed her mistress' hand and held onto it tightly. A dark-skinned man with a bushy moustache, a stubble of beard, and a patch over one eye, suddenly appeared in the open window.

"What have we here?" the man sneered. "Hand over your money and jewels."

"Please, don't harm the women," Father Diaz pleaded.

"Shut up, priest. I'll have that money pouch at your waist." The robber turned to Ana Vasquez. "Your jewels."

Father Diaz handed over the small leather pouch attached to the rope belt girding his waist. It contained only a few silver pesos. With trembling fingers Ana unfastened the pearl neckless she wore, and the two gold bracelets adorning her wrists. The robber demanded the emerald ring on her left hand.

"No, please, it is my wedding ring," Ana begged.

The man barked, "Give it to me or I'll take it. You won't need it now. Your husband is dead."

Ana gasped, and screamed, "No!"

The man reached inside the carriage trying to grab Ana's hand, but Sesasi placed her hand atop his to stop him, and gently removed Ana's precious ring, handing it to the robber. The bandit turned his attention to Bella. "What have you got, little girl?"

He had seen Bella thrust the two velvet pouches she had been holding, one with the gold coins and the other with the rosary, behind her back. She clung fearfully to Father Diaz' arm.

"Please, leave the child alone," Father Diaz asked. "She has just received her First Communion."

The robber stuck a pistol through the window and pointed the gun at Father Diaz' head. "Whatever you are trying to hide, girl, give it to me, or the fat priest dies."

Bella reached behind her back and produced the two pouches. There was a look of fear, but also defiance in her dark eyes as she handed her presents to the bandit. He opened the pouches, and when he saw the gold coins, a wicked smile spread across his face. Satisfied that he had taken all of the valuables the carriage contained, he withdrew. Soon the sound of horses' hooves thundering on the hard ground receded into the distance.

Deeming it safe to exit the carriage, Father Diaz pried Bella's hands from around his arm and clambered down from the coach. The Don's horse was gone, as were the horses of the ranch hands. One of the Mesti-zos sat leaning against the rear wheel of the carriage, groaning and holding his bleeding arm. The other ranch hand lay unmoving, sprawled in the dust. Father Diaz spotted the Don lying face down on the road forty feet ahead of the carriage horses. As Father Diaz approached, he heard a low moan coming from the Don.

"Sesasi! Come quick! Help me! The Don is alive, but I fear he is gravely injured."

Sesasi jumped down from the carriage, followed immediately by Bella, who was too quick for her mother to stop. Bella froze at the sight of the dead and injured men. She had never before been exposed to any manner of violence. She watched Father Diaz and Sesasi approach her father and ran after them.

Father Diaz knelt in the roadway next to the Don and gently turned him over. There was a spreading bloodstain on the left side of his ruffled white shirt. The Don opened his eyes halfway. "Ana? My daughter?"

"I'm right here, Papa," Bella said. Never before had she ever addressed him by any other name than Father, but seeing him wounded and vulnerable made her feel as though she could be more familiar. "Mama is safe in the carriage."

"We must get him into the carriage and back to the hacienda," Sesasi remarked.

"We need a clean cloth, something to staunch the blood," Father Diaz said, looking around as though somehow such a cloth would mysteriously appear.

"Use this," Bella said, already stripping off her Communion dress. Underneath she wore only a simple linen shift. The priest wadded the dress and placed it over the Don's wound. He put the Don's hand atop the cloth and said gently, "Keep pressure on this, my Don." He turned to Sesasi. "Help me carry him to the carriage."

The Don was a little above average height, but slim of build. It was all the priest and housemaid could manage to lift and carry him to the carriage. Bella retrieved her father's sword, which he had dropped on the road when he was shot. As she picked up the rapier, she noticed two bandits lying dead at the side of the road. Spooked at the sight, she hurried after Father Diaz and Sesasi.

They laid the Don on the seat where Bella and Father Diaz had been sitting. Ana dropped to her knees on the carriage floor next to her wounded husband. Sesasi knelt beside her mistress to render whatever assistance she could.

The injured ranch hand was also helped into the carriage. The carriage driver had been killed, and lay slumped on the bench seat. Father Diaz lugubriously ascended to the driver's perch, and Bella, still clutching the rapier, climbed up after him, preferring to ride with the priest than inside the carriage which was filled with moaning and smelled of blood. The priest released the brake, took the reins, and drove the coach the rest of the way to Casa Del Rio Verde, arriving after dark.

CHAPTER FIVE

Servants met the carriage in front of the house and carried the Don to his bedchamber. One of the ranch hands was dispatched to quickly ride ten miles to a neighboring hacienda owned by a doctor. An examination of the Don by Father Diaz and Ana determined that the pistol ball was still imbedded in Don Vasquez' side. There was no exit wound. The ball had to come out before infection set in. The Don had also suffered a head injury when he fell from his horse. A large bruise above his right eye was starting to swell and turning black and blue. Ana was worried her husband would not survive the night. Nevertheless, she steeled herself to tend to her husband as best she could. Sesasi had some experience treating minor injuries; there were always injuries to the hired hands on a busy rancho like Casa Del Rio Verde. She heated water and brought clean cloths to use as bandages to the Don's room.

Bella, still wearing only her linen shift, sat in the hallway outside her father's chamber, her back against the wall, hugging her drawn-up knees. She had witnessed robbery, mayhem, and death on the day of her First Communion. She could not understand why God would allow such violence to come upon her family. She was a stoic child, never cried when she fell or got a cut or a scrape, but she cried that evening, and did not even understand why. It was not for her father's wounds that she shed tears, and not for the loss of her First Communion presents from her grandfather and uncle, although she had taken a fancy to the ivory-beaded rosary. Even at seven-years-old she understood that they were just things and could be replaced. It was the unsettling events of the robbery, terrifying, but in another way, exhilarating, that led to tears streaming down her cheeks.

Bella had carried her father's sword into the house from the carriage, and it lay on the floor at her side apart from its scabbard. In her child's mind she thought that if the robbers followed them home and broke into the house, she could use the rapier to defend herself. She had often admired the sword with its ornate hilt and long, slender blade, as it hung above the fireplace in her father's library. When her father wore it dangling over his left hip, she thought it made the Don appear especially dashing.

It was after midnight by the time the ranch hand returned with the doctor from the neighboring hacienda. They were greeted by half a dozen ranch hands armed with lanterns and muskets, posted to stand guard in front of the casa. The doctor was quickly escorted into the house and upstairs to the Don's room. He passed by a sleeping Bella, who was curled in a ball on the hallway floor, her little girl's hand grasping the handle of her father's rapier. The sight of her made him smile. He entered the bedroom and found the Don in and out of consciousness, and pale from loss of blood. His quickly assessed that the pistol ball had to come out.

He placed a rolled up cloth between the Don's teeth, and enlisted Father Diaz, Ana, and Sesasi to hold the Don down while he operated.

The doctor sterilized a small, sharp knife in a candle flame and made an incision over the wound. Don Vasquez writhed in agony as the knife cut into his flesh, but Father Diaz and the two women held him firmly. The wounded man moaned and groaned as the doctor probed into the wound with a small tong, finally extracting the round lead pistol ball. Don Vasquez passed out, and the doctor liberally poured brandy from a flask in his medical bag over the wound. He stitched the wound closed and covered it with clean cloths held in place by strips of linen wrapped around the Don's waist.

Sesasi left the room and found Bella sound asleep just outside the bed chamber door. She pried Bella's finger's from around the sword's handle and scooped up the child to carry her to bed.

"Is Father okay?" Bella mumbled, half awake.

"Yes, my sweet girl. The doctor came and, thank God, your father will live."

"What about the other man, Pedro? He was hurt, too." Bella knew most of the ranch hands by name.

"Oh, we were so worried about your father, we forgot about Pedro. After I tuck you into bed I will ask the doctor to look at him, too." Sesasi carried Bella into her room, helped her out of her linen shift and into a nightgown. Bella really needed a bath, but it was way too late for that.

"Sesi, will you come back and sleep with me?" Sesi was Bella's pet name for her favorite housemaid.

"Are you afraid the robbers might come to the casa?" Sesasi asked. "There are armed men guarding downstairs. You have nothing to fear, little one."

"Father's sword is on the floor."

"Yes, I saw. I will return it to the library. Sleep now, precious one." Sesasi leaned down and kissed Bella's forehead. Bella yawned, closed her eyes, and fell back asleep before Sesasi had even left the room.

In the morning Bella hesitantly opened the door to her father's bedchamber and peeked inside. She wanted to see for herself that he was alive and well. He was not well, but was alive. He was pale and looked weak. A bandage was wrapped around his forehead. His eyes were open, and when he saw his daughter's face peering around the edge of the wooden door, he beckoned for her to enter.

"How are you, Father?" Bella asked timidly, as she approached the bed. "I picked up your sword and brought it home for you."

"Did you? Thank you. It is the sword I carried as a captain in the army. I was afraid I had lost it." The Don's usually stern expression softened. He had had little to do with his daughter during her seven years. He looked Bella over closely, and gave ger a weak smile. That was a first.

Never one to be shy for long, Bella boldly said, "You wish I was a boy, don't you Father."

The Don sighed. "I wanted a son, yes, but I got a daughter, a beautiful daughter. Come here, Child."

Bella inched her way closer to the side of the bed. Her father took her small hand in his large one, and drawing her hand to his lips, kissed the back of her hand. "You are a good girl, Isabella. Now run downstairs to your breakfast."

Bella left the room, closing the door behind her. A broad smile graced her face. It was the first time her father had shown her any affection, and it made her feel warm and good inside. She scampered down to the kitchen where the cook was making scrambled eggs and tortillas for breakfast.

It did not take long for word of the attack on the Vasquez family to spread. Late in the afternoon of the day following the robbery, Philip and

Miguel Navarro rode to Casa Del Rio Verde accompanied by a band of armed men. Bella saw the riders approach from the window of her room on the second floor. She hurried downstairs to greet her grandfather and uncle on the broad veranda that spanned the width of the house.

"Are you okay, my child? Were you hurt?" Philip Navarro scooped his granddaughter up in his arms and kissed her soft cheek.

"No, Poppa, but the bad men stole my rosary and my gold coins."

"As long as you were not harmed, little one. Those things can be replaced." He set Bella down as Ana came out of the house.

"Father," she said, embracing Philip and then in turn, her brother, Miguel.

"We will hunt those men down," Miguel told his sister. "We shall not rest until everyone of them is shot or hanged."

"Come, Daughter, take us to see Domingo." Philip Navarro turned to one of the men in his party and said, "Julio, join us."

Bella stared as the man her grandfather had called Julio gracefully dismounted his big gray gelding. He was a tall, rangy man sporting a goatee. He was armed with a rapier similar to her father's, and four pistols thrust through a broad sash around his waist. There was a hard look about the man, enhanced by a prominent scar on the left side of his face. He ascended the steps to the veranda, and snatched off his sombrero before entering the house. As he passed by Bella, he paused and looked down for a moment at the child. His eyes were dark and penetrating, a little scary, but Bella stared back at him defiantly, and a brief smile passed his lips as he turned away and entered the casa.

Ana led her father, brother, and the third man up the stairs to the Don's chambers. Bella followed, keeping a discrete distance. Don Vasquez was awake. He grimaced as he sat up, leaning back against the headboard.

"We will hunt those men down." Miguel repeated the vow he had made to Ana.

"Do you recognize this man?" Philip asked, laying his hand on the arm of the man he called Julio.

Don Vasquez squinted and looked the man over. He did seem familiar.

"Julio Higuera, Excellency," the man said, taking a step forward.

"Sergeant Higuera? Is that really you?"

"Yes, my Captain," Higuera replied. "It has been many years."

"What have you been doing in those years. I seem to recall you left the army just before I did."

"That is true, Captain." The man shrugged. "I have been doing this and that. I have worked at breaking horses, guarding payrolls and such."

"Julio is going to help us track those bandits," Miguel put in.

"Perhaps you would like a position on my hacienda," Don Vasquez said. "I am in need of a reliable foreman."

"I would like that very much."

"That was my hope," Philip said. "Julio has done some guard work for me, and has been a steady, solid worker. I knew you would need help while you heal, and I immediately thought of Julio as an ideal foreman for your operation."

"It is agreed then," Don Vasquez extended his hand; he and Julio sealed the arrangement with a handshake.

When the men left the Don's bedchamber, Bella was standing just outside the door, leaning against the wall. "You are certainly a curious child, are you not?" Philip placed his hand under his granddaughter's chin and tilted her face up so he could look into her dark eyes.

"Yes, Poppa, I like to know things. Are you going to hunt those bad men."

"I am a little old to go chasing bandits across the countryside. Your uncle will lead the posse. I will remain at your house for a few days. Would you like that?"

"Yes, Poppa, I would like that very much. We can go for a ride. I have a pony. Momma and Father gave her to me just last week. Her name is Esmerelda, but I call her Esme. Come down to the stables and you can see her." Bella turned her attention to Julio Higuera. "You are going to be the new foreman. I am pleased to meet you, Señor Higuera. I am Isabella, but everyone calls me Bella." Bella stuck her hand out to shake.

Taken aback, the new foreman stared at the precocious child for a moment, but then took her delicate hand into his heavily callused one. "The pleasure is mine, Señorita Isabella Vasquez." He made a slight bow of his head and followed Philip and Miguel downstairs.

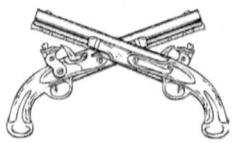

CHAPTER SIX

The Navarros dined with Ana that evening, and Julio Higuera was invited to join them. The talk at the table was all about hunting down the robbers. Miguel vowed he would recover his sister's jewelry, if possible, and particularly her wedding ring. Bella, as usual when there were guests at the casa, was served dinner in the kitchen, which she much preferred. She would rather take meals with Sesasi, Father Diaz, and the other servants than sit at the long dining table where she had to be silent, seen but not heard. She liked the simple but tasty food the cook prepared for the ranch hands and servants better than the fancy fare served in the dining room.

In the morning, before Bella was awake, Miguel Navarro led his troop of men out to scour the countryside for the robbers. Philip had posted a reward of one thousand silver pesos for information leading to the bandits apprehension.

When Bella awoke, she joined her mother and grandfather for breakfast, and then took "Poppa" by the hand and led him to the stables. She proudly showed off her roan and white painted pony and the tack, including a sidesaddle just her size.

"I haven't ridden Esme yet," Bella said, feeding the pony a lump of sugar filched from the breakfast table. "Will you help me saddle her?"

"Of course," Philip replied with a smile. After saddling the pony and fitting the bit in her mouth, he lifted Bella up and set her on the saddle. "Hook your right leg over the horn," he told her.

"Why can't I ride the way you and father do?"

"It isn't ladylike."

"But I'm not a lady. I'm a girl. I feel like I'm going to fall off."

"You will be fine. Just keep your leg over the saddle horn, and hold onto the reins. Shall we take a ride around the corral?"

"The corral? Let's ride out to see the cows."

Philip laughed. "Practice in the corral for a while, and then if you are doing well, we might take a ride out to see your father's cattle." He walked next to the pony to make sure Bella did not fall off. She was nervous at first, but after a few turns around the corral, she got the hang of riding sidesaddle. Philip saddled and mounted his big bay gelding. He towered over Bella. Looking down at her upturned face, he smiled and asked, "Shall we go?" He started out at a slow trot, and Bella's pony followed closely behind. A ranch hand opened the gate for them. Continuing to maintain a slow pace, grandfather and granddaughter rode side-by-side out to the nearest pasture, a broad swath of low grassy hills, sparsely dotted with scrub oaks. At least two hundred head of prime beef cattle grazed in the field.

In one corner of the pasture, a lone bull was enthusiastically mounting a heifer. "Poppa, what are those two cows doing?" Bella naively asked.

Philip hesitated a moment and then replied, "The big one on the other's back is a male, a bull. The other is a female. They are making a calf. In that way your father's herd continues to grow."

Bella's eyes grew wide. "Poppa, is that how people babies are made?"

"You are too young to be thinking about such things, Child. Come, let us ride back to the stable. It will soon be time for lunch."

At the stable, Philip helped Bella remove her pony's saddle and bridle. He handed her a curry brush. "Every time you ride, Child, you must rub down your horse and brush her. In that way she will stay strong and healthy." He demonstrated on his own horse how it was to be done. Afterward, they went to the house where the cook had prepared a light lunch, served outdoors on the veranda.

Miguel and his party did not return for three days, but when they did there was a triumphal smile on his face. He presented his sister, Ana, with her wedding ring that had been taken in the robbery. He was unable to recover her bracelets and necklace, and the velvet pouch with Bella's gold doubloons was also gone, but he proudly handed his niece her ivory-beaded rosary.

"We were tipped off that the robbers were hiding in a narrow canyon," Miguel related to Don Vasquez. "We came at them from two sides. There was a lot of shooting, but only one of my men suffered a minor wound. We killed all but two of the bandits. There were eight highwaymen in all. The two we captured, we hung. Other loot was also recovered, and has been sent back to Mexico City. We will try to find the true owners of those items."

"Uncle Miguel, I am glad you killed those bad men who shot Father and Pedro and killed Alejandro. What if you cannot find the real owners?" Bella asked. She was standing uninvited behind her grandfather and uncle in her father's bedchamber.

Miguel turned to her and, trying not to smile, said, "You should not be in here, Child, with this talk of shooting and hanging. You always want to know what is happening, do you not? Such an inquisitive child. If the true owners cannot be found, the money and jewels will be sent to the King in Spain."

"If there was money, how do you know some was not mine? The robbers could have mixed it with other money."

"You are a bright girl, Bella. Your coins were specially marked, each one stamped with the year it was minted, one for each of your seven years. When I return to Mexico City, I will examine the gold coins we found. If I find seven with year marking starting with 1765, then I will set them aside for you."

"Thank you for finding my rosary. When I pray it, I will always remember my First Communion, but maybe I will remember the robbery, too."

"Do you pray your rosary every night, Child?" Bella's grandfather asked.

"How could I, Poppa? I did not have my rosary until now."

Philip affectionately tosseled her dark curls. "If you say your rosary every night before you sleep, the Virgin will keep you safe."

That night, after her bath, Bella knelt on the floor at her bedside and prayed the rosary. The ritual of repeating the strings of Our Fathers and Hail Marys made little sense to her, but she liked the tactile feel of the smooth ivory beads, and the weight of the small, solid gold crucifix attached to the end. Her mind wandered at times, and she would lose count of the Hail Marys. She wondered if it was a sin to daydream while praying. She resolved to ask Father Diaz about it in the morning. She yawned and fell asleep before finishing her prayers, still on her knees, her head resting on the bedding. Sesasi found her when she looked in to make sure Bella was tucked in. The Indian housemaid loved Bella almost as though she were her own child. She smiled, and lifting the girl, gently laid her in the bed, with Bella still clutching the rosary in her small fist. Sesasi pried open Bella's hand and set the rosary on the nightstand next to the silver candleholder. She leaned down, kissed Bella on the forehead, blew out the candle, and quietly left the room.

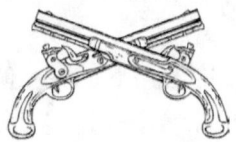

CHAPTER SEVEN

Julio Higuera moved into the bunkhouse, formerly the original casa on the hacienda built before the Don acquired the property. The house had been converted to a bunkhouse for the ranch hands once the newer, big house was finished. Julio had proved his worth in the hunt for the robbers, killing two of the bandits himself during the shootout. He was a no-nonsense, somewhat taciturn man. His management style on the ranch was the same as it had been when he was a sergeant in the army. He barked orders, expecting them to be carried out immediately. Given full authority over the ranch hands, he quickly determined which hands were hard workers, and which ones were slackers. In short order he dismissed the lazy men and hired replacements.

Initially, Bella thought the new foreman was scary. Frequently he was in the stables seeing to the Don's personal horses when Bella visited Esme.

One time when she encountered Julio at the stables, she worked up the nerve to ask his help saddling her pony.

"If you can't saddle your own horse, you have no business riding," he replied sharply and turned away.

Bella could scarcely believe a hired hand would refuse to help her. She was the Don's daughter, his only child. She was accustomed to servants doing everything for her, from preparing her meals, to making up her bed, to bathing her before bedtime. She stood with her hands planted on her hips and stared at the foreman, but he ignored her. Finally, she threw the blanket over the pony's back, and took the saddle down from the stall rail. The saddle was heavy, and it was a struggle, but eventually she managed to get it onto Esme's back. Fortunately, the pony was docile. The little mare waited patiently as Bella fitted the bridle over the pony's head, setting the bit between her teeth.

Even though the pony was small, Bella still had difficulty mounting her. She was used to getting a boost up from one of the ranch hands, but the only hand present was Julio Higuera. He was whistling with his back to Bella, and she was hesitant to again ask his help. He will just say if I cannot mount my own horse, I have no business riding, she thought. Finally, she dragged a wooden box into the stall, stood atop it, and hoisted herself onto the saddle.

"Come, girl, let's go for a ride." Bella lightly touched the pony's flank with the heel of her shoe, and Esme trotted out of the stall and into the corral. When Bella got to the gate, she leaned down and unlatched it, almost falling off Esme's back. Neglecting to close the gate behind her, she guided the pony across the expanse of lawn in front of the casa, heading out to explore the hacienda. Unbeknownst to her, the Don was watching from the upstairs window. He was frowning. It was the first time he had been out of bed after being wounded, and he was not pleased by what he saw, Bella riding off unaccompanied and neglecting to close and latch the gate.

It was a little scary riding out alone. It was the first time Bella had taken the pony out by herself. The only other time she had ridden outside the corral, she had been with her grandfather. Bella rode into the hills rising behind the house, moving at a plodding pace, the pony's only gait. Esme was twenty years old, no longer a youngster, not that she had ever been frisky. Her sedate nature made her ideal for a young novice rider.

Bella rode for about a mile. Scores of brown cattle spread out across the hillsides were grazing on lush green grass. Bella followed a path worn by years of ranch hands riding out to tend the herd. She spotted two deer feeding amid the herd and reined in Esme to watch. As she started to move ahead once again, there was a warning rattle. Coiled in the middle of the path was a large rattlesnake, its head raised, baring venomous fangs. Esme panicked, reared up, and Bella tumbled out of the saddle, landing on her rump on the hard-packed dirt.

Esme bolted, moving at a surprisingly quick trot for a tired old pony, headed back toward the corral, leaving Bella sitting on the ground with the snake not six feet away. She held perfectly still, too frightened to move. She stared at the rattler, it stared back at her. Finally, Bella won the staring contest. The snake slowly uncoiled and slithered away into the tall grass.

Bella stood and brushed the dust from the back of her long skirt. Her bottom hurt; it had been a hard fall, and she had twisted her ankle. Her pony was gone, so there was nothing for it but to walk back to the house. It was hot, and she was sweating, limping painfully with each step. She crested a low hill and saw the casa in the distance. It looked like ten miles to her instead of one.

Suddenly a horse and rider appeared, headed in her direction. As the man drew closer, Bella saw that it was Julio Higuera. He reined in his dappled gelding next to her.

"Can't stay on your horse?" he asked with an amused smile.

"There was a snake," Bella replied.

"Are you injured? Did the snake bite you?"

"No, but I hurt my bottom and my ankle."

Julio nodded. "Your pony returned without you. Come." He leaned down, extending his hand. Bella grabbed it, and he lifted her effortlessly. Settling her on the saddle in front of him, he turned the horse for home.

When they reached the corral, Esme was standing outside the closed gate, looking longingly at the stables, wishing for the comfort and safety of her stall. Julio set Bella on the ground.

"Unlatch the gate, Girl. You must always latch the gate after you. You left it open. Had I not been here, horses might have escaped."

"But I hurt my ankle," Bella complained. "It hurts to stand on it. I want to go in the house so Sesi can fix it."

"Not until you curry your horse. Look at her. She is in a lather, and she is frightened. You tend the horse before you tend yourself."

Bella was about to protest, but she knew Julio was right. She recalled her grandfather telling her the same thing. She nodded and unlatched the gate. She grabbed Esme's reins and, for show putting on an exaggerated limp, led the pony into her stall. If she was expecting sympathy from Julio, she got none. She removed Esme's bridle, and the saddle, which was as much a struggle to get off as it had been to put on, and then used a towel to wipe down the horse's flanks. She picked up the curry brush and went over every inch of the pony until Esme was clean and calm. Bella put an armload of fresh hay in the feed trough, and patted her pony's neck affectionately. She realized she had forgotten all about her own aches and pains while tending her horse. She resolved to bring Esme an apple and a couple lumps of sugar after dinner.

Bella turned to leave the stall and ran directly into Julio, who was silently standing behind her, watching her care for her pony. "Oh," she said, taken by surprise.

"You need a regular saddle, not that ridiculous sidesaddle rig," he said.

"But I am a girl," Bella protested. "Grandfather said riding like a man is not ladylike."

"That may be so, but you might not have fallen when your horse spooked if you had been sitting a regular saddle with your feet in the stirrups. The land out here is not some grassy park in the city. It can be dangerous, as you found out today." With that, he turned away and headed for the bunkhouse. That was quite a stream of words for Julio. Bella's opinion of him softened a little. Afterall, he had come looking for her out on the grazing fields, and he rode her home, saving a long and painful walk.

Bella limped toward the house, and was met at the door by Sesasi. "Your father wants to see you in his room. When you are finished, I will tend your ankle." The housemaid shook her head. "I have never seen a child get as dirty as you. Shoo now, go, see your father. I will draw a bath."

Bella climbed the stairs to the second floor, again walking with an exaggerated limp, fearing she was in trouble, and wishing for mercy from the Don. She rapped lightly on the heavy wooden door, hoping there would be no answer.

"Enter," her father called.

When Bella pushed open the door, she found her father in his dressing gown, seated in a highbacked chair by the open window.

"You went out riding by yourself."

"Yes, Father, I ..."

"And you left the corral gate unlatched."

"I'm sorry, Father. Julio, Señor Higuera, I mean ..."

"You are not to ride by yourself, do you understand?"

"Yes, Father, but ..."

"No buts. Come here, daughter."

Hesitantly, Bella crossed the room to her father's chair.

"Look at you, Girl. You are filthy from head to feet."

"There was a snake, and I fell off Esme's back. Señor Higuera found me and rode me back to the corral."

"So I saw. Bend over my knee."

"But Father, I fell on my bottom. I have a bruise."

"Then this will hurt just a little more."

Bella hesitated a moment, but understood she could not talk her way out of being punished. She leaned across her father's knee and gritted her teeth. The Don swatted her behind once, not too hard really, but for effect Bella let out a yowl. "That is for riding alone." He gave her another swat. "That is for leaving the gate unlatched. The next time it will be my belt, not my hand. Now go and get cleaned up."

Bella hurried out of the room, closing the door after her. It is not fair, she thought, as she went in search of Sesasi. No one ever told me I could not ride alone. She knew leaving the gate unlatched was wrong. The punishment for that was fair, but to be swatted for something she had never been told was not allowed seemed the height of injustice.

After soaking in a warm bath, and being scrubbed head to toe by Sesasi, Bella felt much better. Sesasi wrapped a strip of cloth soaked in a pungent ointment, an old Native American remedy for sprains, tightly around Bella's ankle. There was a saucer-sized black and blue bruise on her hip. Well, she thought philosophically, it could have been worse. The snake could have bitten me.

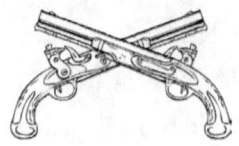

CHAPTER EIGHT

Bella did not go to the stable the next day. Her hip was too sore to think about riding. The following day, however, she remembered she owed Esme an apple and lumps of sugar. She stuck two apples and a handful of sugar cubes in the pockets of her skirt and walked to the stables. The ointment Sesasi had applied to her ankle had worked remarkably well. There was hardly any soreness remaining. Even her bruised hip felt a little better. When she reached her pony's stall, Bella was amazed to find a small, gaucho-style saddle perched on the stall's wall where her old sidesaddle used to be. She looked around, but did not see Julio anywhere. She knew the saddle had to have come from him. She fed Esme the two apples and all of the sugar, and patted the pony's neck lovingly.

Despite her father's order that she not ride alone, Bella decided to try out the new saddle. It was even heavier than the sidesaddle, and she struggled to lift it from the rail and get it onto Esme's back. She remembered

Julio telling her that if you cannot saddle your own horse, you have no business riding. Finally, she got Esme saddled, cinched up tight, and bridled. Hiking up her long skirt, she raised her left leg and slipped her foot into the stirrup. She grabbed the saddle horn and hoisted herself onto the saddle, throwing her right leg over the pony's back. Immediately she knew that was the way a horse should be ridden, and vowed to herself she would never ride sidesaddle again. She touched her heels to Esme's flanks, and the pony trotted out of the stall and into the corral.

It was a beautiful day, warm and sunny under a cloudless sky. Bella trotted her mount around the corral a few times, but the lure of open ground was too tempting to ignore. She glanced at the window of her father's room. She did not see the Don. She rode to the gate, leaned down and unlatched it. Once through the gate, she dismounted, re-latched the gate, and climbed back onto the pony. I am sure it will be all right if I stay close to the house, she told herself, and again touched her heels to the pony's flank to get the old girl moving.

Before she had gone far enough to get herself into trouble, Julio, on his way back from inspecting the herds, rode up beside her. He reined in his horse and gave Bella an approving nod.

"Thank you for the saddle," Bella said. "This is a much better way to ride." She hesitated a moment. "Señor Higuera, would you ride with me? Father forbade me from riding alone."

"So I heard. He asked me to keep an eye on you." He gave Bella a half smile. In truth he was becoming fond of the impish girl. "Yes, I will ride with you, but you must do something for me in return."

"What?" Bella asked, a little warily, afraid he might ask her to muck out the stalls or perform some other onerous task.

"Señor Higuera sounds a little too formal for a ranch hand. Call me Julio."

Bella thought for a moment. "I call the other hands by their first names, but you are the foreman. What if I call you Sergeant Julio? You were a sergeant when my father was a captain in the army."

His smile broadened. "Yes, I like that. Sergeant Julio will do just fine. Shall we go for a ride?"

Bouncing up and down on her bruised hip was not fun, but Bella was nevertheless thrilled to be out riding on such a lovely day. Sitting astride the pony felt much more secure than perched sidesaddle. From time-to-time, she glanced up at Julio riding next to her. He sat easy in the saddle, completely relaxed. His horse moved at a walk, keeping pace with Esme's plodding gait. They rode much farther than Bella had ever been on the hacienda. It was eye-opening to realize that all of the property, just about as far as the eye could see, belonged to her father.

At noon, as they headed back toward the house, they stopped at a small stream and dismounted to allow the horses to drink. Julio removed a leather-covered canteen from his saddle and offered Bella a drink. "You need a canteen of your own," he told her. "When you go riding, you should take food and water with you." He reached into his saddlebag and pulled out a package wrapped in paper, two cornmeal tortillas rolled around pieces of grilled beef. He handed one to Bella, and together they sat on the coarse grass in the shade of a scrub oak, eating their lunch.

Julio Higuera had never married and had no children, at least none that he was aware of. He had never felt completely comfortable around children, but had taken a liking to Bella. She was a beautiful little girl, with her dimpled chin, big brown eyes, and long black curls. He liked that she was brave and adventurous.

"Sergeant Julio, what was it like in the army with my father?" Bella asked, wiping her greasy hands on her skirt.

"Your father was a good captain," he replied, smiling.

"Did you fight in many battles?"

Julio laughed. "Battles are fought between armies. We had a few skirmishes with bandits."

"Is that how you got this?" Bella reached up and touched the scar on the left side of his face.

"I fought a duel with a bandit. He was a good swordsman, but I was better. He gave me this cut on my face, but I ran him through."

"Did it hurt when you got cut? It hurts when I get cuts or bruises."

"Yes, it hurt, but when you are in a fight for your life, you do not think about pain. You must stay focused on the fight. If you do not, you will die."

Bella sat quietly for a minute. "Sergeant Julio, will you teach me how to use a sword?"

He laughed. "How old are you, Child? You are a girl, and you are much too young to learn to fence, even if you were a boy."

"Fence? You mean like building the corral?"

He laughed again. "No, fencing with swords. That is what dueling is called."

"I am almost eight," Bella said. "And why shouldn't girls know how to fight? I was really scared when those bandits robbed Momma and shot Father. If I had a sword, I would have stabbed the man who stole Momma's jewelry."

"I believe you would have. Come, let us head back to the stables. Father Diaz will be wondering where you have been off to."

The priest was standing by the corral, leaning against the wooden railing when Bella and Julio returned from their long ride. He was pretending to frown, but like the grizzled former sergeant, he, too, was immensely fond of his pupil. "We were supposed to have lessons this afternoon," he said, trying unsuccessfully to sound gruff. He was surprised to see Bella astride her pony instead of riding sidesaddle. It seemed a little unladylike, with her skirt hiked above her knees and her lower legs bared, but her broad grin was infectious.

"Sorry, Father. I will be there right after I curry Esme."

"I am afraid I have gotten you in trouble," Julio commented.

"Not at all. Can we ride again tomorrow?"

"Perhaps, we will see."

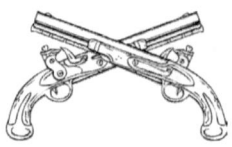

Chapter Nine

The following morning, when Bella went to the stables, she found two wooden swords, one her size and the other considerably longer, leaning against the outside wall of Esme's stall. The shorter sword had her name carved into the wooden blade. She smiled. When she turned around, she found Julio standing in the entrance to the stable leaning against the doorframe, his arms folded across his chest.

Bella looked at him and then at the swords again. "You are going to teach me sword fighting?"

"It is what you wanted, is it not?"

"It does not seem fair," she said pouting. "You are so much bigger than me, and your arms are longer, and your sword is longer. How am I supposed to fight you?"

"Ah, I see. You planned to only fight other eight-year-old girls. Then there is no point in my teaching you, since you are the only young girl on the hacienda." A broad smile spread across his face. "Señorita Bella, even when you are a grown woman, any man you oppose will probably be taller than you, with a greater reach. Success in sword fighting does not rely on the length of your arm, or your blade, but on your skill, speed, agility, and determination. When you face an opponent, you must mentally picture yourself defeating him. There can be no doubt in your mind, no hesitancy. You must always fight as though your life is on the line because it is. Any man who engages you will try to kill you. You must be prepared to kill him first. Now, do you want to begin, or are you too frightened?"

"I am not afraid," Bella replied, even though there was a knot in her stomach, and her mouth felt cottony.

"Good. Shall we practice behind the stables? And Señorita Bella, please do not mention to your father that I am instructing you in fencing. I like my job here and want to keep it."

"And I do not want a spanking," Bella replied, grinning mischievously. Sharing a secret with Sergeant Julio helped dissipate some of her nervousness.

Bella, carrying her wooden sword, and Julio toting his, went out the rear exit of the stables, away from prying eyes. Behind the stable was a wide patch of hard packed dirt, an ideal spot for the lessons.

"When you engage, stand like this." Julio demonstrated the stance, left foot forward, facing ahead, right foot back a little, turned to the outside, knees slightly bent. "In this way, you can easily move forward to attack, or back to retreat. Hold your sword thus." Bella was gripping the handle of the sword tightly, her fingers wrapped completely around the smooth, sanded handle. "Open your hand, lay the grip across your palm, and grip it with your fingers, not so stiffly, but not too loosely, either. You must be able to move the blade to meet your opponent's blade. Use your wrist to change the angle of the blade, not your whole arm. You can tighten your grip to keep your opponent from disarming you, and when you thrust it is important to keep a firm grip. You will come to understand these things as you practice. Now watch this."

Julio assumed the stance he had demonstrated, holding his wooden sword in front of him at about a forty-five degree angle. He moved forward with graceful speed and made a thrust into the air. He moved back and then forward again, constantly moving his sword as though he was engaged in a duel. "You see?"

"I think so," Bella replied, nervousness creeping back into her voice.

"Then *en garde*, as the French say." He squared off facing Bella. Even though it was merely a lesson and they were using blunt wooden swords, her knees felt wobbly. Julio towered over her. She positioned herself as he had shown her and raised her sword. His attack was lightning quick, and with a flick of his wrist he disarmed her, sending her sword flying. He poked her in the tummy, rather hard, with the rounded tip of his sword. Bella was stunned, and on the verge of tears.

"Do you want me to build you up with false hope, or teach you swordsmanship?" Julio asked a little harshly to get her attention. His voice softened. "You must understand Bellita, this is serious business. If I were a bandit, I would have run you through with a real sword, and you would be dead. Now, have you had enough, or do you want to pick up your sword and try again?"

Bella blinked back tears. "Try again." No one had ever called her Bellita before, but the endearment warmed her heart. She walked to her sword and, picking it up, turned to face Sergeant Julio again.

His next attack was deliberately slower, and purposefully more obvious. Bella swatted his blade away with her much shorter sword.

"Good, good, but not such large movements. When you parry ..."

"What is parry?"

"It is when you deflect your opponent's blade. Use smaller motions, just enough to move your enemy's blade aside. When your moves are too broad, you open yourself to a second attack, like this." Julio, with a flip of his wrist, swung his blade around Bella's, and again poked her in the tummy.

"Ow," she said, frowning.

"Believe me, being poked with a wooden sword is nothing compared to being skewered on a real one. Again."

Julio and Bella practiced for nearly an hour, until her arm was so tired she could scarcely hold the sword up. "That is enough for today, Bellita. You are doing well. I think you might make a decent swordsman someday."

"Swordswoman," Bella corrected him with a grin. She scampered off to find Father Diaz for the day's other lessons.

That night, as Sesasi undressed Bella for her bath, she asked, "Bella, Love, what are these red marks on your stomach? I hope you do not have the measles."

Bella hesitated a moment. "If I tell you something, you must swear not to tell Father. Señor Higuera is teaching me how to fight with swords."

"With swords?" Sesasi was alarmed.

"Wooden swords. They are not sharp. You must promise not to tell anyone. Señor Higuera says I might be a great swordswoman someday."

"Is that a good idea?"

"Sesasi, when those robbers attacked us, I was helpless. I want to know how to defend myself, and Mother, and you, too."

Sesasi smiled at Bella. "Okay, Great Swordswoman, get into the tub. I swear I have never seen a child with such talent for getting dirty as you."

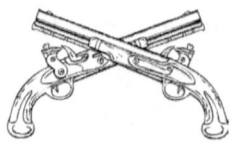

CHAPTER TEN

Father Diaz was dead. For ten years he had been Bella's teacher, and during that time he had opened up the world to her, literature, history, politics, mathematics, and science. He had instilled in her enough Latin that she could understand what was being said at Mass, and he planted in her a desire to learn everything she could about the world around her. She had become an avid reader, devouring almost a book a week from her father's library. She had free rein to use the books he had bought to impress others, but never opened himself.

Bella found that the priest had died when she went to his cottage for her daily lessons. He was lying in peaceful eternal rest in his bed, his face serene in death, having passed quietly in his sleep. Bella had just turned fourteen, and with Father Diaz' passing her formal education ended. Even as a young teenager she had nearly surpassed her teacher in learning. Father Diaz had given up on writing his history of Mexico's indigenous peoples and had taken to drinking too much wine in the evenings. Bella was not prone to crying; her demeanor was generally relaxed regardless the circumstances, but she wept inconsolably when she discovered the priest's cold, pale corpse. She loved Father Diaz dearly. He had been more than her teacher, he was her priest, her confidant, her confessor, but most of all her friend. She gathered all of his notes and writings and packed them away in a trunk, with the thought that one day she might finish his work.

Rather than transport his body to Mexico City to be interred in the cemetery there, Father Diaz was laid to rest on a low hilltop overlooking the hacienda where he had faithfully served. Bella, dressed in black, wept again as the wooden coffin was lowered into the grave. A wooden cross, carved with his name and the date of his passing served as a marker: Fr. Fernando Diaz; 19 June 1779. He had never revealed the date of his birth. It seemed to Bella that a grander monument should have been erected for the man she loved much more deeply than even her own father. She realized, however, that Father Diaz had been a simple Dominican Friar, and perhaps a simple wooden cross was sufficient for one such as he. Bella placed a large bouquet of wildflowers she had gathered atop the mound of fresh dirt.

There were other changes at Casa Del Rio Verde. Bella's father, Don Domingo Vasquez was sixty-two years old and not in good health. His wound from seven years earlier, received during the robbery that occurred on the day of Bella's First Communion, had never fully healed properly. He walked with the use of a cane topped with an ivory handle carved in the form of an eagle's head. More and more of the day-to-day operations of the rancho were entrusted to Julio Higuera, now manager of the hacienda.

Bella's mother, Ana Navarro Vasquez, was still a young woman, only in her mid-thirties, but she had never been able to conceive again after giving birth to Bella. She was kept busy running the household, managing the servants, and arranging dinners and parties for important guests who came to the Don seeking favors, or to conduct business.

As for Bella, she had grown more beautiful with each passing year. Even at fourteen, she was tall and willowy, only a head shorter than her father. She had begun to develop feminine curves, and business associates of her father, men with sons in their late teens or early twenties, had begun to take notice of her, thinking an alliance through marriage with the Don would be to their advantage. No longer relegated to an early dinner in the kitchen with the servants, Bella was always present at the lavish dinners given by her parents, and she added sparkling conversation and occasionally riotous laughter to what were otherwise rather dull affairs. When there was a party to attend, at Casa Del Rio Verde or a neighboring hacienda, Bella was usually the Belle of the Ball.

That is not to say she no longer had a wild streak. She loved to roam the vast hills and fields of her father's hacienda astride her horse, a dappled gray mare named Gabriella—Gabby for short. Bella had outgrown her pony, Esme, who still resided in her stall, content to nosh hay and the occasional carrot or apple. By the time Bella was ten, her father had given up trying to restrict her roaming the hacienda alone. He had also became aware of her fencing lessons with Julio Higuera. Initially disapproving, when he one day surreptitiously watched her practice—Bella was twelve at the time—the Don realized how amazingly good she was. After four years of intense training, she had graduated from wooden swords to a blunt tipped epee. As in her academic lessons with Father Diaz, she had surpassed her fencing instructor. Her skill, speed, and agility were second to none. She could penetrate Sergeant Julio's defenses at will, and without fail deflected his every attack.

It was not only at sword work that Bella had become adept. One afternoon, shortly after turning fourteen, she had wandered into the stables and found Sergeant Julio perched on a stool cleaning his pistols. He always carried a brace of pistols thrust through the sash he wore around his waist. He had a reputation as a deadly pistol shot. Fascinated, Bella sat on a bale of hay and watched as Julio meticulously cleaned, oiled, and reloaded his pistols. He had fired a few practice shots at jackrabbits earlier in the day while out riding amid the cattle, killing two with two shots from horseback at twenty yards. Julio looked up from his work, gave Bella a smile and a nod, and continued reloading the pistols.

"Teach me to shoot," Bella said.

Julio looked at her, hesitating a moment. "You should ask your father."

"He will say no." Bella was always of the opinion it was better to ask forgiveness than permission. "If I had asked him if I could to learn to fence, he would have refused. Now, he knows you have been teaching me for six years behind his back, and all he said was that he thought I was 'pretty good' with a sword."

"I would say you are more than just pretty good," Julio said, laughing. "I suppose if you are to become an infamous desperado, you should know how to shoot."

It was Bella's turn to laugh. "I am not going to become a desperado, but I do want to learn to shoot a pistol."

"Saddle Gabby and we will go for a ride." Julio stood, tucked his pistols in his sash, and went to saddle his horse. Bella had Gabby ready to ride in short order. She sat astride her horse waiting in the corral for Julio to join her. Since she had long before given up riding sidesaddle, Sesasi had taken several of Bella's billowy skirts and stitched a double seam up the middle, turning them into gaucho pants, more modest than hiking her skirts up above her knees. She wore a sombrero, similar to the one Julio wore, and a short, waist-length jacket, fancily embroidered, over her blouse.

When Julio joined her, she led the way out of the corral, leaning down to unlatch the gate. He re-latched it behind them. They rode into the hills behind the casa, passing by the grave of Father Diaz, now covered in grass. The cross still marked the spot, and as they rode by, Bella nodded her head in silent tribute to her friend and teacher.

When they reached an open area, where there were no cattle nearby to shoot accidently, they dismounted and tethered the horses to a scrub oak where there was plenty of grass for them to graze. Julio removed a canvas sack that had been tied to the back of his saddle and drew out a wooden box made of English walnut and fitted with brass hinges and locks. Bella, curious, watched as he opened the box. Inside were nestled a pair of pistols and accessories, a powder flask, a leather pouch filled with lead balls, small cloth patches, a silver vial of oil, and cleaning implements.

"These are dueling pistols," Julio explained. "I believe they are of English make. I received them from a wealthy land owner in partial payment for services I rendered a long time ago, before coming to work for your father. These are very unusual pistols. The barrels are rifled."

"What does that mean?" Bella asked, admiring the graceful lines of the two guns.

"Most pistols are smoothbores, like a musket, not very accurate except at close range. Look here at the muzzle. You see the grooves cut into the inside of the barrel, that is rifling. It causes the ball to spin as it flies through the air. This makes them much more accurate, even at longer distances. They will get dirty quicker, however, so they must be cleaned more often. Watch, I will show you how to load them."

Bella leaned in close, carefully observing as Julio poured a measured amount of gun powder down the barrels. He then rammed a lead ball, wrapped in a greased patch, down each of the barrels. "This is the cock, or hammer," he explained, as he pulled back the arm holding a piece of flint in its jaws. Bella thought the graceful curved tail looked a bit like a rooster's tail, and wondered if that was where it got its name.

"This is the frizzen." He raised a metal piece with a roughened surface that faced the cock. "You pour a bit of powder into this small pan and close the frizzen. When you pull the trigger, the hammer falls causing the flint to scrape the frizzen. That makes sparks which ignite the gunpowder in the pan and then the powder inside the barrel through this touch hole.

"It seems complicated," Bella commented. "It takes a long time to load. Using a sword is a lot simpler."

Julio laughed. "You are right, pistols are slow to load, and a sword is much quicker. That is why I always carry two pistols, sometimes four." He laughed. "But you do not want to bring a sword to a gunfight. Now, let us see what you can do." He handed her one of the loaded pistols.

"What should I shoot at?" Bella was a little nervous holding the pistol.

"You see that big dirt clod? Aim at it. Line up the front sight with the notch at the rear and also the target. Pull back the hammer, and pull the trigger."

The dirt clod was about fifty feet away. Bella held the pistol at arm's length. It was heavy, but felt good in her hand. She jerked the trigger, and the gun went off; a cloud of white smoke hanging in the air obscured the dirt clod. "Did I hit it?" she asked.

"No, but you scared it pretty good," Julio replied, laughing. He handed her the second pistol. "Try again, and pull the trigger smoothly. Do not jerk it."

Bella cocked the hammer, aligned the sights, and squeezed the trigger more gently.

"Good, you were very close that time, just a little low. Reload the guns and try again. The next time, aim a little higher."

"You want *me* to load the guns?"

"Are you always going to have a servant around to load your pistols for you? Do you even bathe yourself yet?"

"Yes, I bathe myself now," Bella replied, and could not keep from laughing. It was a subject Julio had teased her about for years. Up until a year or so earlier, Sesasi had always dressed and undressed her, bathed her, washed her hair, and dried her afterward.

Under Julio's supervision, she reloaded and primed the pistols. Adjusting her aim, she hit the dirt clod on her next try, sending chunks of dirt and rock flying, and then hit it again with the second pistol.

Julio shook his head. "Señorita Bella, you are a natural. Do it again, so I do not believe it was an accident you hit the target twice."

Bella reloaded the guns and shot each one again, and then yet one more time. By then the dirt clod had been reduced to dust, and it was becoming difficult to ram the lead balls down the barrels due to gunpowder fouling in the rifling.

Again, Julio shook his head, amazed at how quickly his young pupil had grasped loading and shooting a flintlock pistol. "Come, let us ride back to the stables and I will teach you how to clean the pistols."

Once the barrels were scrubbed clean by Bella, under Julio's supervision, with a bristle brush soaked in oil, and the outsides of the barrels were wiped down with an oily cloth, Julio placed the dueling pistols back in the fitted wooden case.

"Can we shoot them again sometime?" Bella asked eagerly. She had been thrilled with the shooting lesson. It was so satisfying to hit what she aimed at.

Julio smiled at her. "Yes, anytime you like you may shoot *your* pistols." He thrust the wooden case into her hands.

Bella's jaw dropped and her eyes grew wide. "Mine? Really?" she asked, hardly able to believe Julio was giving them to her.

He shrugged. "Call it an early Christmas present."

Bella set the wooden box on a bale of hay and threw her arms around the rangy manager of her father's rancho. She hugged him fiercely and then stood on her toes and kissed his bristly cheek. "Thank you, thank you, thank you," she said. "They are beautiful, and I promise I will take good care of them."

"You might not want to tell your father I gave them to you."

Bella laughed. "It will be our secret. Is there a safe place I can keep them here in the stables?"

"Yes, come, I will show you." Julio led Bella into the tack room. There was a locked cabinet attached to the wall where a few tools and other hardware odds and ends were stored. He unlocked the cabinet and placed the boxed pistol set on a shelf. After relocking the cabinet, he handed Bella the key. "Now only you will be able to open it."

Bella hugged him again, and skipped off to the house, her hands stained with gunshot residue and oil, a broad smile on her face.

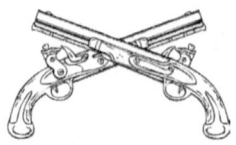

CHAPTER ELEVEN

By the time Bella turned sixteen, friends and business associates of her father, and their wives, were regularly bringing their sons to Casa Del Rio Verde. It was like flies to honey, or bees to roses. Young men from eighteen or nineteen, to men approaching their thirties, came to woo lovely Isabella Vasquez. She was indeed a rare beauty, tall and slender, with waves of black hair falling nearly to her waist. Her dark eyes, set in a heart-shaped face, were beguiling; her laughter was music. Unquestionably she was the prettiest girl in the entire region. Bella had no interest in marrying any of the young men who came seeking her hand.

She thought a few of her suitors handsome, but even the good looking young men she found dull and uninteresting. Their fawning attention was annoying. She much preferred to be riding Gabby at a gallop across the fields and hills of her father's hacienda, than sitting at a dinner table trying to make conversation with some young man and his parents on subjects that held no interest for her,

Bella continued to practice fencing several times a week with Julio Higuera, even though she had surpassed him in skill. Their roles had been reversed. She was now teaching him. On a trip to Mexico City, Bella had found a book on the art of sword play written by an Italian. It was widely acknowledged that the French and the Italians were masters in the art of fencing, even though the two national styles differed. The book was in Italian, but Bella was able to glean the gist of what was written. It helped that the volume was profusely illustrated with detailed drawings. She relentlessly practiced techniques she had picked up in the book, and shared what she was learning with Julio.

"Señorita Bella, I swear there is no man in all of Mexico your equal with a sword," Julio proclaimed after an exhausting workout one hot afternoon. Bella's speed and agility never ceased to amaze him.

She also continued to practice with her pistols every chance she got. Her father eventually discovered that Julio had given Bella the pistols, and he was very angry. He threatened to take them away from her, and was determined to let Julio go.

"No, Father," Bella pleaded. "It is not his fault. I made him teach me how to shoot."

"No, Don Vasquez, your daughter did not *make* me do anything," Julio said. "She asked me to teach her, and I thought to myself, why should a young woman not know how to defend herself? You have seen her ability with a sword. She is an equally capable pistol shot. I will go, if that is your wish, but do not punish Bella for using the talents given her by God."

"Father, please let me show you that I know how to shoot. When we were robbed on the highway, when I was seven, I was terrified. Now, I am no longer afraid."

Don Vasquez glared at his daughter. It was dismaying. He wanted her to be a proper young lady, marry one of her suitors, provide him with grandchildren, a grandson who would eventually take over Casa Del Rio Verde, but all she wanted to do was to ride around like a crazy gaucho. There had to be an end to it.

"Fine," Don Vasquez said, pulling a large silver coin out of his pocket. He walked across the lawn in front of the house to the wooden fence, and set the coin upright on edge, wedged into a split in the top of a fencepost. He returned to Bella who was standing about thirty-five feet from the fence. "Hit that coin twice, and you may keep the pistols." In the Don's estimation it was an impossible shot. Bella's father was certain that no one could hit a target that small from that distance except by pure accident. It would take a miracle to hit it twice.

Don Vasquez stood by smugly confident that Bella would miss, have to forfeit her guns, and that he would finally be able to force her to become domesticated. He was so sure of the outcome, he did not notice the amused look on Julio's face.

Bella was nervous as she loaded the two pistols, sensing her father's motives behind the challenge. So much was riding on her marksmanship. She envisioned him taking away the pistols, forbidding her to continue fencing, and forcing her to return to riding sidesaddle in a lady-like manner. But Julio, standing next to her, said in a low voice, "My Bellita, you can do this." He had not called her Bellita in a number of years, but hearing him say it again brought a smile to her face, and a measure of calmness to her mind.

Bella stood sideways to the fencepost, as though in a duel. It was how Julio had taught her to stand, providing a smaller target to her opponent than facing him head on. She cocked her pistol, extended her arm, and tried to set aside all distractions. As she took aim, she envisioned only hitting the target, the silver coin, but her hand trembled a little as disturbing thoughts tried to worm their way into her mind, disrupting her concentration. Had she used too much powder? Too little? Variations in the amount of powder could throw off the point of impact, hitting below the target, or missing above it. The target was so small there was no margin for error. She closed her eyes for a moment to calm herself, and exerting all of her willpower, banished all doubts. When she opened her eyes, her hand was steady, and the silver coin looked the size of a dinner plate. She aligned the sights, and gently squeezed the trigger. The coin flew from its perch, and although the cloud of smoke obscured Bella's vision, she was certain she had hit her mark.

Julio ran and recovered the coin from the dusty ground of the corral where it had landed. There was a deep impression in the center of the coin. He set it back on the fence post, and after he moved away from the line of fire, Bella's second shot with the other pistol ended with similar result.

Don Vasquez stared at his daughter, stunned, amazed, and had he been willing to admit it, also with a measure of pride. Never had he seen any man shoot with such accuracy. Never had he imagined anyone could be able of hitting so small a mark from such a distance with a pistol. It would have been a feat of marksmanship to do it with a rifle.

"So, Father, I can keep the pistols?" Bella asked.

Her father shook his head, not to say no, but in amazement. His only comment was, "You should have been a boy."

"Do you still want me to leave?" Julio asked, as the Don turned toward the house.

With a dismissive wave of his hand, Don Vasquez said, "Get back to work."

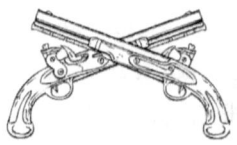

CHAPTER TWELVE

One of Bella's more persistent suiters was a young man of twenty-four named Francisco Alfaro Moreno. He was the son of a banker in Mexico City, and was following in his father's footsteps, working as a junior executive in his father's bank. He was not tall, only a few inches taller than Bella, and he tended toward being a little on the heavy side, especially for a young man, the result of too little exercise and too many hours sitting behind a desk, that and a love of good food and wine. He was, nevertheless, reasonably handsome with wavy dark hair and a thin, dapper moustache. He fancied that he had smoldering eyes, or so he told Bella one evening after dinner as they strolled the grounds in front of the casa. She was not sure what he meant by that remark. If he thought the way he looked at her with his dark, half-lidded eyes would entice her into marrying him, he was sadly mistaken. She thought him a bit of a pompous ass, but walked with him to please her father.

Don Vasquez believed the younger Moreno would be an ideal match for his daughter. His father was a wealthy man, and Francisco was his only son. There was a younger daughter, Celia, around Bella's age, but the son was the heir. The Moreno family had the added advantage of being Iberian born. Only Celia had been born in Mexico. A connection through marriage such as this could only help the Don in his own business interests. There would never be a problem securing a loan. Since Francisco lived and worked in the city, it would mean that Bella would have to give up her wild lifestyle, no more galloping around the countryside, no more fencing or pistol shooting. Francisco seemed to be a strong willed young man, perhaps the one to finally tame Isabella Vasquez.

Francisco visited Casa Del Rio Verde often, first with his father and mother, Fernando and Maria, but then more frequently alone, driven in a carriage to the hacienda by armed servants. He deemed the ride too long to travel on horseback, and feared the ever present danger of bandits on the highway. He usually arrived a little before dinner time on Sunday afternoons, often unannounced. On some visits he had to wait, passing time with the Don and Ana Vasquez, because Bella was out riding Gabby.

On one such visit, after waiting for over an hour, Francisco was appalled when Bella tripped gayly into the house wearing her divided shirt and gaucho-style jacket and sombrero. Her cheeks were fetchingly pink, windburned from a hard ride on a windy day, and there were bits of straw from the stables stuck in her tangled hair after currying and feeding Gabby. Her two pistols were proudly thrust through a sash tied around her slender waist.

"Señorita Vasquez, have you been out herding cattle, or perhaps robbing banks?" he asked mockingly. "You are soon to be seventeen and will wed. You should behave in a more lady-like manner." He administered that admonishment right in front of her parents, and to add to the insult, the Don was smiling approvingly.

Bella stopped in her tracks, the joy of her afternoon ride gone in an instant. She turned to Ana and said, "Mother, I am feeling unwell. I apologize, but I will not be down for dinner. Please ask Sesasi to draw my bath and bring something to eat to my room." With that, Bella flounced up the stairs without so much as a look back.

In her room, Bella fumed, pacing back and forth as she shed her riding clothes. "Soon to be wed indeed," she muttered, pulling off her supple gloves. "Behave in a lady-like manner," she grumbled, stepping out of her skirt. "If that pompous fool thinks ..."

There was a sharp rapping on her bedroom door. "Bella, it is I, your mother. I wish to speak to you."

"Come in, Mother. It is not locked."

Bella was unlacing her blouse as the door opened and Ana entered the room. "Bella, dearest, bathe and put on a pretty dress. Come down for dinner. Francisco traveled all the way from the city to see you."

"I will not," Bella replied. "I do not love him. I do not even like him, and I certainly will never marry a man such as he."

"This afternoon he asked your father for your hand."

"Well, he cannot have my hand or any other part of me."

"Your father has already agreed that you will marry Francisco."

Bella froze, her blouse half off. "What?"

"Your father thinks Francisco will be a good match for you."

"You mean he thinks it will be a good match for him, for father. Well, I will not marry him, not now, not ever, and I am going downstairs right now to tell him so." Bella slipped her blouse back on and tied it closed. She stepped back into her divided skirt.

"Bella, no, wait," her mother begged.

Bella, ignoring her mother, brushed past her as she left her room. In bare feet, she tromped down the stairs to the library where the Don and Francisco Moreno were having a glass of sherry to seal the deal, to celebrate the arranged marriage. The door was slightly ajar, and Bella could hear the men talking and laughing. She stormed into the room, slamming the heavy wooden door wide open, banging it into the wall. She stood just inside the room, glaring at her father and her erstwhile suitor.

"What is the meaning of this?" she demanded. "Mother said you have arranged for me to marry this ... this man." Man was not the word that almost escaped her lips. "I will *not* marry him, *never*."

"I am your father, and you will do as I say," the Don said angrily. "You will marry Francisco, and that is the end of it."

"I will not! You cannot force me! I will marry whom I choose, if I choose to marry at all."

Don Vasquez crossed the room, and without warning, slapped Bella hard across the face, hard enough to cause her to stumble backwards a step. "I am your father, and you will do as I say."

She stared at her father in shock and disbelief. Other than a few, half-hearted swats on the rear when she had been a mischievous child, she had never been struck, and certainly not on the face. Her cheek felt hot, and it stung. She did not cry—Bella was not a crier—and would not have given her father the satisfaction of showing tears under any circumstances. Fuming, she turned on her heel and stomped out of the room.

"Go to your room," the Don called after her. "And stay there until I say you may leave. There will be no dinner for you tonight."

As Bella ascended the stairs, she overheard her father apologizing to Francisco Moreno for his daughter's rude, unruly behavior. She went to her room; it was where she was headed anyway. Her mother was gone. Bella slammed the door shut and paced the room. She stopped at her dressing table and looked at her face in the mirror. Her left cheek was fiery red. It hurt, but what hurt more was that her father would force her into marriage against her will, that he would strike her, his only child.

She heard a key turning in the door lock. He is locking me in, she told herself. She rattled the doorknob, and tried to open the door, but it was locked from the outside. She did not even have a key to unlock it from her side. She had never locked the door.

"I should have taken my pistols downstairs," she muttered under her breath. "I should have shot them both." After fuming for another half hour, her anger slowly dissipated. She knew that her words were just angry talk. Of course she would never shoot her father, or even Francisco Moreno, the pompous pig, no matter how much they had offended her. But what am I going to do, she wondered. One thing she would not do was marry Francisco Moreno.

She was dirty and needed a bath, but was locked in her room, probably until morning. Still clothed, she stretched out on her bed, staring up at the ceiling. Suddenly it came to her. She knew what she had to do. I cannot stay or I will be forced to marry that ass, and so I must leave, she told herself. She rose from the bed and went to her window. It was a long way to the ground. She began knotting her bed linens together to make a rope. She could hear talking and laughing downstairs. She knew she would have to wait until everyone was in bed asleep before making her escape.

In the meanwhile, Bella took inventory of her possessions. She had an old leather satchel that had belonged to Father Diaz. She stuffed it with spare undergarments and another blouse. She put into the bag her ivory rosary and seven gold coins, replacements from her Uncle Miguel for the ones taken in the robbery on her First Communion day. It was all the money she had. Until now she had had no need of money. Her father provided for all of her needs.

There was a small clasp knife in the drawer of her dressing table; it had also belonged to Father Diaz. She tucked the knife into the pocket of her skirt. She packed her comb and hairbrush in the satchel. She had her pistols. Luckily her father had not thought to take them away from her. They were loaded, but the flask of gunpowder and extra lead balls were locked in the storage cabinet in the tack room. Well, she thought,

I have the key. The last items to go into the bag were a few candles and sulfur matches. All that remained was to wait.

Bella again stretched out atop her mattress, now devoid of the bed linens. She was determined to remain awake, but the day had been long and stressful. She was tired from a long afternoon ride, and soon her eyelids grew heavy.

Part Two

FLIGHT

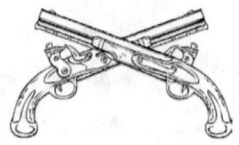

CHAPTER THIRTEEN

Bella awoke with a start. The house was completely silent. The candle in the silver holder on the nightstand had burned to a stub, telling her that morning was approaching. She arose and put on clean stockings, her riding boots, and waistcoat. Tucking her pistols into her sash, and slinging the leather satchel over her shoulder, she threw the ersatz rope out the window, one end tied securely to a bedpost. She climbed down from her room, dropping lightly to the ground the final five feet.

She was hungry, not having eaten since luncheon the previous day. She crept around to the rear of the house and slipped through a side door into the courtyard where the kitchen was located. A stack of stale corn tortillas was on the table where the cook prepared the meals. A pot of cold leftover shredded beef and beans, dinner for the servants and ranch hands, was on the stove. Bella wrapped meat and beans into the tortillas, rolling them into slim cylinders. She stuffed one in her mouth, and placed the others in dried corn husks before slipping them into the satchel.

She was about to exit the same way she entered when she thought of something else she wanted. Slipping off her boots so as not to make noise walking on the tiled floor, she entered the house through the rear entrance. Carrying her boots and walking silently in stocking feet, she entered her father's library and took down his rapier in its scabbard from the pegs where it hung above the fireplace. She attached the belt frog that held the scabbard to her sash and left the house through the front door.

The sky in the east was starting to fade from black night to pre-dawn gray as she walked to the stables. She had to make haste. After retrieving the accouterments for her pistols from the locked cabinet, she saddled and bridled Gabby. The horse snorted loudly at being disturbed so early.

"Shh," Bella said softly, rubbing her horse's muzzle and stroking her neck. "That's a good girl."

Bella took the reins and walked Gabby out of the stable and out of the corral, being sure to re-close the gate and latch it. Just as she was slipping the toe of her boot into the stirrup, a voice behind her called out, "Bella? Is that you? Where are you going at this hour?"

She turned to find Julio Higuera walking toward her, having come down from the bunkhouse to get an early start on the day. She froze. What could she tell him? The truth. She could not lie to her friend.

"My dear Julio, I am leaving. I must. Father insists I marry that foolish young man, Francisco Moreno. I cannot, I will not do that."

Surprised and dismayed, Julio asked, "But Bellita, where will you go? When will you come back?"

"I do not know where I will go, but I cannot stay here. Probably I will not come back, not while Father is alive. You are my dearest friend, Sergeant Julio. Please do not tell my father that you saw me leave. He will send you to find me, and send other men. Look for me east or west. I tell you this because I trust you. I will go north.

"Bella, Bella ..."

"I must go now, my friend. Please do not try to stop me."

"No, I will not stop you, and I will be sure not to find you, if you do not wish to be found, but I will miss you sorely, my Bellita. I love you, Girl. To me you are the daughter I never had." He hesitated a moment and then added, "I could go with you."

"I love you, too, Julio. But you will serve me better by throwing father's men off my trail, and I do not have time to wait while you get ready." Bella enveloped him in a fierce hug, and tears seldom shed flowed from her eyes at parting from the man who had been more like a father to her than the Don had ever been. He kissed her forehead, and she kissed him back on his bristly cheek.

"Take this," Julio said, and pulling a dagger in its sheath from the top of his boot, thrust the knife into her hand. "And these. It is all I have right now." He reached into his pocket and produced a handful of silver pesos.

"Thank you," Bella said, and with tears still streaming down her cheeks, mounted Gabby. She put heels to the horse's flanks and thundered out of the yard, no longer caring about disturbing her parents or the servants. She rode east at a gallop, deliberately leaving a trail for anyone sent to track her. The sky was taking on a pinkish tinge ahead of her. As she reached a low hill half a mile from the house, she stopped and took one last look back over her shoulder at the only home she had ever known. With a knot in her stomach, she turned and headed north, not knowing where she would end up, but certain she would never see Casa Del Rio Verde and her parents again.

After a while Bella crossed a stream and continued riding north all morning, putting as much distance between herself and Casa Del Rio Verde as she could. She was certain her father would send men after her and was determined that under no circumstances would she return home. Home. Her father's vast hacienda was no longer home. She no longer had a home, but she had her freedom. She was alone, and had never before felt so alone and lonely. Several times she almost lost her nerve and was tempted to turn back, but the idea of being locked in a loveless marriage to a man she despised spurred her on. She wished Julio was with her, but had she waited for him to get ready, she might have been found out by her father. Perhaps Julio will come to join me one day, she thought. I told him I was riding north. As she slowed Gabby to a walk to give the horse a rest, she daydreamed of Julio finding her, and together they would travel to someplace where her father would never look for her. I would marry a man like Julio, she told herself, but maybe not one as old as him. Julio was only a few years younger than the Don, not only old enough to be her father, but old enough to be her grandfather.

At noon she stopped at a stream to let Gabby drink and to fill her canteen. She had passed two small farming villages, giving them wide berth. She did not want anyone giving her father's men leads if they made inquiries. Giving Gabby and herself a rest, she sat in the shade of a scrub oak and ate the remaining two meat-filled tortillas. She wondered where she would spend the night. She had never slept anywhere but in her own soft bed. I am certain to find a nice inn somewhere, she naively thought.

There was still daylight left, so she remounted Gabby and continued on. The terrain grew a little more rugged, and to Bella's dismay, she had not spotted another village all afternoon. She rode past a few isolated farms, run down, hardscrabble plots, where tattered people eked out a subsistence living from the stubbornly unyielding land. Ragged children watched with wide, vacant eyes as she rode past. One child pointed a finger at her and hollered, "Bandita." He thinks I am a bandit, Bella thought, amused at the very notion, but then after all, she was displaying a brace of pistols, and a long rapier dangled over her left hip.

The sun set beyond a line of distant hills, and Bella had not found a place to stay for the night. She settled down close to another small stream. She had nothing to eat, but was able to build a small fire using dead mesquite branches. The fire provided a measure of comfort, offset by the discomfort of the hard ground. She rested her head on Gabby's saddle, and covered herself with the horse's blanket. The temperature dropped quickly once the sun was down. She was dirty, and sweaty as the day had been quite warm. Used to taking a bath daily, she was miserable and could not get comfortable, tossing and turning for what seemed like hours. Just as she was finally drifting off to sleep, coyotes began to yip in the distance as the nearly full moon rose. The coyote song was joined by the howling of wolves coming from the opposite direction. Bella kept her loaded pistols close at hand.

When she awoke, the sun was just peeking over the tops of distant mountains. Bella stood and stretched to get the kinks out of her back. With nothing to eat, she had to be satisfied with drinking her fill from the stream and refilling her canteen. For a brief moment she flirted with the notion of turning back, but recalling the image of Francisco Moreno's soft belly stretching the fabric of his shirt, and his smug, know-it-all grin, steeled her reserve. She mounted Gabby and continued riding north, putting more miles between her and Casa Del Rio Verde.

At midday she finally spotted another village far off in the distance. If her father's men came looking for her there, she would deal with that if it happened. She trotted Gabby into the cluster of adobe buildings, keeping to the middle of the dusty lane that ran through the middle of the town. She passed a bodega selling food and general merchandise. There was a small church and a cantina, which was not much to look at from the outside, and even shabbier inside, as Bella discovered after tying Gabby to a hitching post and passing through the swinging door.

As her eyes adjusted to the dimly lit interior, she saw half a dozen rough-looking patrons, all men, and all staring at her. A man behind the bar was also giving her the eye. Four of the men were sitting at a table playing cards, and two more stood leaning against a crude wooden bar. The man behind the bar was pouring drinks for the customers. Bella was a strange sight in such a place, a pretty, sixteen-year-old girl, finely dressed despite the trail dust on her clothing. What made her appearance especially unusual, however, was the brace of pistols secured in her sash, and the fancy sword dangling from her hip.

Bella hesitated for a moment, standing just inside the door, wondering whether there was another and perhaps friendlier place to get something to eat, and hopefully a room for the night. She had seen no other such place in the village, and doubted there was one hidden away somewhere. She took a deep breath and crossed the room, passing by the card players, whose heads turned to follow her progress to the bar.

"Yes, Señorita?" The barman asked. He was a rotund man, grizzled, with fat stubbly cheeks, a wrinkled brow, and a preposterous moustache.

"Can I get something to eat here?" Despite her reservations about the cantina, hunger gnawed at Bella's empty belly.

The barkeep stared at her for a minute with small, piggy eyes, and then hollered over his shoulder, "Maria, bring food." Without asking, he poured beer from a wooden tap into a semi-clean glass and set the glass on the bar in front of Bella. Apparently beer was what was available to drink, or harder liquor. She was accustomed to having a small glass of wine at dinner at home, but had only tried beer a few times. She was not particularly fond of beer, but it would serve to wash down the trail dust she had swallowed and whatever passed for food in such a place.

She carried the glass to an empty table as far from the card players as she could get. A minute later a woman, as fat as the bartender, emerged from a backroom carrying a plate with beans, a slab of gristly meat, and a few tortillas. She set the food on the table in front of Bella, and stood staring at the strange girl. The card players were also staring at her, as was the man behind the bar.

"Is everyone going to watch me eat?" Bella asked, addressing the entire room. The men at the card table returned to their game, the woman went back to the kitchen, and the barkeep pretended to be polishing glasses.

Surreptitiously all of the men continued to steal glances in Bella's direction. Ravenous, she chose to ignore the other patrons. She ate what of the meat was edible, wolfed down the beans and tortillas, drank the beer, and felt better with a full stomach.

Chapter Fourteen

Finished with her meal, Bella went back to the bar and laid one of the large silver pesos Julio had given her on the counter. "Will that cover my meal?" she asked. She had no notion of what things should cost.

The bartender's eyes grew wide and he snatched up the coin greedily. A couple of copper pesos would have sufficed.

"Is there anywhere I can get a room for the night and a place to stable my horse?"

Before the barman could respond, one of the two men who had been drinking at the bar sidled closer to Bella's left side, uncomfortably close. "I have a place you can sleep tonight," he said, laughing.

"No, thank you." Bella moved away a few feet, but the man moved also, still crowding her. The second man moved from the other end of the bar and came up on Bella's right.

The second man asked, "What is such a pretty Señorita doing here all alone? Any more silver where that came from?"

Both men were dressed in tattered pants and shirts, and both were as grizzled as the barkeep, although much leaner. They were looking at Bella hungrily, and the men playing cards, stopped their game to watch, perhaps hoping to get in on the action. The first man grabbed Bella's left wrist, holding her tightly, and for an instant Bella froze in fear. She may have been somewhat naïve, but not so naïve as to not know what these men intended. Her mother had never discussed relations between men and women with her, but Sesasi had warned Bella more than once to beware of men and their evil desires. Julio Higuera had once told her that because of her great beauty, men might try to take advantage of her, and for that reason had encouraged her to always carry her pistols when out riding alone.

Bella jerked a pistol from her sash, cocking the hammer as she did so. She shoved the muzzle of the pistol into the belly of the man grasping her wrist and pulled the trigger. The sound of the gun shot was muffled by contact with the man's flesh. He released her wrist and staggered backwards, looking down stupidly at the expanding stain of blood spreading across his raggedy shirt. He swayed for a moment and then fell onto his back.

There was stunned silence for a minute inside the cantina. "You bitch!" the second man at the bar shouted, drawing a long, wicked-looking knife. Bella stepped away and drew her father's sword. The man with the knife backed off a few feet. Two of the men at the card table started to stand, but Bella pulled her other pistol with her left hand and pointed it in their direction. Wisely, they sat back down.

"You killed that man," the bartender said. Gut shot, the man was not dead, but likely would be soon.

Holding her sword and pistol at the ready, Bella backed toward the door. The barman suddenly dipped down behind the counter and came up with a cutdown, double-barreled fowling piece. He was cocking both hammers when Bella raised her pistol and fired, striking the man in the center of his forehead. He fell, dead before he hit the floor. Bella turned and fled through the swinging cantina door. She untied Gabby and quickly mounted her horse. Leaning low over the horse's neck, she dug her heels into Gabby's flanks, and the horse leapt forward, galloping down the dusty road. A shot rang out behind her, but Bella did not look back. She rode Gabby hard until she was well clear of the village.

Finally slowing to a trot, she looked over her shoulder, but saw no one pursuing her. She reined Gabby in and sat still in the saddle, breathing heavily. Her heart was still pounding. The enormity of what she had done, killing two men, hit her hard. Feeling sick to her stomach, she leaned aside and threw up the miserable meal she had just eaten. The words of the little boy at the farm she had passed, "Bandita," rang in her ears. Is that what I've become, she asked herself, a bandit? Am I now a murderer? Up until that point, using her weapons to defend herself had only been a theoretical possibility. Now it had become cold reality.

She consoled herself with the thought that she had acted on the likelihood that she would otherwise have been raped, and maybe then murdered, but the sight of the man at the bar, lying on his back, bleeding to death, was completely unsettling. Shooting the barman had been less disturbing. It would have been her lying dead on the cantina floor if he had fired that double-barreled gun. The first man she shot had not even pulled a weapon. She shot him instinctively, without stopping to think about what she was doing. I am a murderer, she told herself, and tears filled her eyes. For sixteen years she had been a good Catholic girl, attending Mass every Sunday, and had gone to confession weekly even though she had no terrible sins to confess. Now she did, and the very thought of telling her sin to a priest sent a chill down her spine. How could such an awful sin ever be forgiven?

Her stomach empty, but with no desire for food, Bella rode on until she found a sheltered spot under an outcropping of rock to spend the night. She reloaded her pistols and built a small fire for warmth, and for whatever solace it could provide. She sat with her back against the cold, hard rock, her knees drawn up, and reviewed in her mind the events of the afternoon. What could she have done differently? Why had she not just paid for the meal and left the cantina peacefully? Perhaps, she eventually thought, what had happened was inevitable. There were six men inside the cantina, seven counting the bartender, and all of them had looked at her lustfully. Had she not defended herself, she was certain horrible things would have happened to her. That thought eased her conscience a little, and she finally fell asleep, sitting up, her head nodded forward on her chest.

When Bella awoke the sky was pre-dawn gray. Her neck was stiff and sore. She stood, stretched, and rolled her neck a few times to get the kinks out. There was no point in building up the fire; she had nothing to cook, nothing to eat. She drank from her canteen, saddled Gabby, and was about to mount the horse when a shot rang out. A pistol ball whizzed past her, striking the rock wall nearby. She saw three mounted men riding hard in her direction, no more than a hundred yards away. She quickly leaped onto Gabby's back and raced off at a full gallop with the men in hot pursuit.

She could not tell whether they were from the village, perhaps the men from the card table, or possibly soldiers. Was she now a wanted woman? That thought flitted through her mind as she rode into a twisting arroyo. Fortunately, Gabby was rested, whereas her pursuers' horses had been ridden hard for a long time. Bella increased the distance between herself and the men chasing her, but they continued to follow.

As she passed a steep, rocky bend in the arroyo, she brought Gabby to a sudden halt. Even astride her horse she would remain hidden from view until the men rounded the curve. Bella drew and cocked her pistols and waited. The thundering beat of horses' hooves pounding the rocky bottom of the dry riverbed grew louder as the men approached. They rounded the turn and quickly reined in their horses when they found themselves facing Bella.

Without a second's hesitation, she fired both pistols, holding one in each hand. Two shots and two of the riders fell from their mounts. The third man fumbled for his pistol, but Bella drew her rapier and charged at him. The man, utterly shocked, managed to draw the pistol, and firing at point-blank range, accomplished the almost impossible feat of completely missing Bella. She drove her sword deep into the man's right shoulder. The pistol dropped from his hand and he stared stupidly at the blade skewering him until Bella withdrew the sword. He slowly slid off his horse, falling to the hard ground.

Bella's first instinct was to turn tail and flee, but a long, low moan from one of the fallen men brought her up short. If she left them, they would die. She wiped the bloody tip of her rapier on the saddle blanket, and returned it to the scabbard. She dismounted, and warily approached the downed men. The first man she examined was dead, shot through the heart. The second man she shot was the one moaning. Her shot, fired from the pistol in her left hand, had taken the man in the right side. He was losing a lot of blood. The third man, stabbed with her sword, was also moaning. Bella decided the man with the gunshot wound was the more seriously injured.

She first relieved all three men of their weapons—pistols and knives—and then retrieved her spare petticoat from her leather satchel. She used the dagger Julio had given her to cut the cloth into strips. She bound the men's wounds the best she could. She did not recognize any of them. They were not men from the cantina, and not soldiers either. The man with the shoulder wound sat up, leaning against a large rock as Bella bandaged his wound. The blade had pierced him clear through, front to back.

"Why do you not leave us to die?" he asked, as Bella knotted the cloth around his wound.

"Why were you chasing me?" Bella answered his question with one of her own. The man was young, probably in his early twenties, and not bad looking, Bella thought.

"Señorita, there is a bounty of one hundred silver pesos on your head. That is a lot of money for men such as myself and my friends. Many more men are searching for you."

Bella's heart sank. Bandita. She was a wanted woman. There was a price on her head. She no longer felt as though she was the innocent, carefree young girl of a few days earlier. She had killed three men and wounded two more. The thought flashed through her mind that leaving her home had been a huge mistake. She should have stayed and married the foolish Francisco Moreno. At least she would not be wanted for murder. Too late for that now. She envisioned a life on the run, constantly hunted, to be either shot down or captured and hung.

To hang me, they will have to catch me, she told herself, and I will not allow that to happen. She stood, sighed, and searched through the three men's saddle bags, woven cloth sacks tied to the backs of their saddles. She found flasks of gun powder and pouches of pistol balls. One bag contained dried beans and a small pot. In another there was a small quantity of jerked meat, goat perhaps, she thought. She took the gun powder and pistol balls, the food and the dead man's canteen. She kept the four pistols that had been shared among the three men. If she were now to be a desperado, she had better be well armed. She left the dead man's musket in its scabbard attached to his saddle. Neither of the surviving men were capable of wielding the long gun in their condition. She helped both wounded men onto their horses.

"Go home," she said. "Tell others not to pursue me or they will end up like him." Bella nodded at the dead man still sprawled in the arroyo.

"Who are you?" the man with the shoulder wound asked, looking at Bella in wonder.

"I am Isabella Vasquez. Now go."

"Isabella Vasquez," the man repeated, shaking his head. That is how her name appeared on wanted posters thereafter.

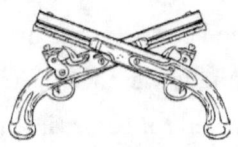

CHAPTER FIFTEEN

Bella continued her journey north, chewing a piece of the tough jerky while she rode. She was not sure why she had picked that direction, other than that she had a notion it was less populated than the southern part of Mexico, or toward either of the two coasts. She knew from her geography lessons with Father Diaz that Spain's dominion extended far to the north of the Rio Grande. She knew there was a very old city, Santa Fe, in the territory called New Mexico. She thought that perhaps she could get lost in the land north of the Rio Grande. She had only a vague notion of the distance from her home to the great border river. She knew it was over six hundred miles, but had no idea how long it might take to get there on horseback. Presently she was much father away from her father's house than she had ever been. She was discovering that the world was a much bigger place than boundaries of the hacienda where she grew up.

That evening as she camped beside a small stream, Bella cooked a meal for the first time in her life. She boiled a handful of beans in the pot she took from one of the men, and added a little salt, also found in one of the saddlebags. She shredded a little of the dried meat to add flavor. Even boiled, the meat was tough, as were the beans—she did not know the beans should have been soaked for some time before cooking. Tough did not matter; she was famished.

A price on my head, she thought, stoking her small campfire with a stick to stir up the flames. She knew that now, even had she wanted to—which she did not—she could never return to her father's house. Wealthy or not, her father could not save her. She would be arrested and hanged if she returned to the hacienda. She had cleaned and loaded the four pistols she recovered from her pursuers as well as her own two guns. At least she had extra weapons, powder and shot for whatever she might face. She lay back, her head resting on Gabby's saddle, staring up at the star-studded sky. She was certain that by then her father would have sent men to look for her, and she hoped Julio had thrown them off her trail by urging that they search east and west.

Julio. The thought of him brought a smile to her face, but also an ache to her heart. She did not realize how much he had meant to her until they were apart. She allowed herself to indulge in a fantasy wherein he came after her, and they set out together to explore the lands north of the Rio Grande. She drifted into sleep and dreamed of galloping across a broad plain, with Julio by her side. She awoke fully expecting to see him hunched by the fire, preparing breakfast for the two of them. Of course he was not there. She sat up and spotted a coyote standing fifty yards away, staring at her. The wily critter trotted off, disappearing into thick brush.

The next several days were uneventful, except for a thunderstorm that swept in from the west. Bella and Gabby took shelter from the storm in a ruinous shack, once a farmer's or perhaps a prospector's hut, long since abandoned. When the storm passed she continued north, and thus far no more men had come after her. Ahead and to the east the Sierra Madre range rose in the not too far distance. She worried about entering the mountains. The terrain looked rugged and forbidding, but west of the range were scattered villages and farms, and after her experience in the cantina, she was leery of passing through places where people might be on the lookout for her. Even if her father's ranch hands were thrown off her track, the men who had pursued her were clearly aware that she was traveling north. She had no idea how far her notoriety might have spread, and so she entered the mountains.

Sticking mostly to canyons, dry river beds, and faint game trails, Bella wound her way between peaks and over mountain passes, always keeping Gabby's nose pointed north as much as possible in the twisting maze that was the Sierra Madre.

Late one afternoon, as she was looking for a place to camp for the night, Bella rounded a bend in an arroyo at the bottom of a canyon and came upon a man squatting by a campfire. Startled, he turned at the sound of Gabby's hooves, stood, grabbed a musket, and aimed it at her. Bella's immediate reaction was to reach for a pistol, but when the man saw that it was only a girl on horseback, he lowered his gun.

Still holding the musket in his right hand, he raised his left in greeting and said something unintelligible in a language Bella did not understand. He was young, in his late twenties Bella guessed, and was handsome, but in a strange way. His longish hair, pulled back in a short ponytail, was the color of straw, and he had a scraggly blonde beard. His eyes were strikingly blue. Bella had never seen anyone with blue eyes before, but knew from books that such people existed. He was tall and rangy, and he had a friendly, easy-going smile. He carried one pistol stuck through a wide leather belt around his waist.

"*Ingles*?" Bella asked.

"American. Alder, John Alder." The year was 1781, and Bella was aware that there was a war going on between England and her colonies in America. The Americans were seeking their independence, and the government in Spain worried that some of her colonies might get the same idea. She had no idea what a man from the east coast of North America was doing so far from home.

"Alder John Alder," Bella repeated, and introduced herself. "Isabella Vasquez."

The man gave her a lopsided grin. "Alder will do just fine."

The only thing Bella understood was the man's name, "Alder," but she intuited that was what he wanted to be called.

He asked her something else that she could not understand, but he made a motion with his hand as though putting food into his mouth, and pointed to a fat hare roasting on a spit over the fire. Bella realized he was inviting her to eat with him. Her first inclination was to decline and keep moving, but the aroma of roasting meat was enticing. For days all she had eaten were beans and jerky, and her supply was nearly exhausted. She had put herself on slim rations for the previous two days.

Bella hesitated a moment, and then warily dismounted. She tethered Gabby to a low shrub, but left her saddled in case a quick getaway was needed. She removed her rapier and hung it from the saddle horn; it was awkward to sit with the sword dangling from her side. Her two pistols were loaded and primed, and there was only one man to be concerned about.

Alder gestured for Bella to take a seat on one of the large rocks near the fire. He could not help staring at her; he had never seen a girl so pretty. Her facial features were perfect, and her dark eyes watching his every move were enticing. Her long, inky black hair fell in waves over her shoulders and down her back. She was young and mysterious. What is a girl such as she doing alone in a God-forsaken place like this, he wondered. She carried a brace of pistols and looked as though she knew what to do with them.

Bella sat quietly perched on the edge of the rock, keeping alert, staying on guard. She watched as the man spooned a generous helping of beans from a pot next to the fire onto a tin plate. He cut a haunch of rabbit and put it on the plate, too, and then brought the plate to her, handing her a silver spoon. She rested the plate on her knees and ate. The beans were soft, tender, and flavorful, and the well-seasoned rabbit seemed like the best thing she had ever eaten.

Alder sat on the opposite side of the fire and ate beans directly from the pot with the wooden spoon he had used to stir them. He could not keep from frequently looking up and staring at the beautiful girl sitting across the fire. She seemed like someone out of a wonderful dream. He gnawed the meat from the hare's ribcage and forelegs, reserving the other meaty haunch in case Bella wanted more, which she did. She smiled and nodded eagerly when he offered it.

"*Gracias,*" she said, handing Alder back the plate after eating every last bite of her dinner.

He had almost no Spanish, and Bella spoke not a word of English, so conversation was impossible, but they watched each other from across the flames, and Alder's easy, friendly smile put Bella somewhat at ease. His almost constant staring at her was a little unsettling, but his look was strictly appreciative of her beauty, not like the lustful stares of the men in the cantina. She had a choice to make, camp there for the night with this stranger, or move on. There was a little twilight glow above the canyon rim, but deep in the arroyo, the shadows were dark and gloomy.

Bella stood and went to Gabby. For a moment Alder was worried that she was going to leave, but he relaxed and let out a sigh of relief as he watched her remove her horse's saddle. She carried the saddle back to her side of the fire and spread the saddle blanket on the hard ground. She sat on the blanket, her back resting against the saddle, and watched as Alder scoured the tin plate and cast iron bean pot with a handful of sand, wondering what his story was, just as he was wondering about hers.

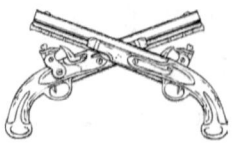

CHAPTER SIXTEEN

John Alder had been a soldier in George Washington's revolutionary army. He enlisted in 1776 soon after the opening shots were fired. He had been a laborer, working at whatever jobs he could find. He had no love for the arrogant British, and the way the Redcoat soldiers paraded through the town as though they owned the place. In a way, he supposed they did. America was a British colony, just as Mexico was a colony of Spain. Alder believed it was high time Americans threw off their colonial masters and formed their own nation. He was filled with fiery zeal until the lack of pay, poor food, shabby uniforms, and the seemingly constant retreating from superior British forces ground him down.

Finally, one day after a skirmish with a company of Hessians, the hated German mercenaries hired by King George to supplement the regular British army, Alder had had enough of the fighting. His company was ordered to retreat once again, but instead of following orders, he hid in a thicket. That decision made him a deserter, and if caught would mean a firing squad. He had no intention of being caught. He waited patiently, practically freezing in his shabby, much-patched blue uniform coat, until both sides in the battle had moved on.

When he was certain that no one else was around, he crept out of hiding. He found a dead Hessian and stripped the man of his boots, which unlike Alder's, were intact and without holes. The boots were a close enough fit, and Alder began walking, headed south. His company had retreated north. As luck would have it, late in the day he encountered a British dispatch rider. He shot the man and took his horse and pistol. Alder continued on, headed south and west. He traveled for days, and weeks, and months, always south, away from the frigid northern winter.

He stole what he needed to survive along the way, a blanket here, a cookpot there, eggs from henhouses, rabbits from hutches, chickens from farmyards. He robbed a general merchandise store in a dusty two-bit town in northern Alabama, crossing the line from deserter and thief to wanted outlaw. He made his way into the Louisiana Territory, crossing the wide Mississippi River on a ferry. Eventually he entered Tejas, or Texas, part of Spain's vast empire, and continued on until he reached the Rio Grande. He swam his horse across the river and entered Old Mexico. A few weeks later, deep inside the Sierra Madre, a beautiful Spanish girl rode into his camp and into his life.

After sitting silently across the campfire for a while, Bella placed her hand over her chest and said, "Bella." She then pointed to the fire and said, "*fuego.*"

Alder wondered for a moment, was she trying to teach him Spanish, or did she want to learn English? He decided to go with the latter. "Fire," he said.

"Fire," Bella repeated, and then she began to point out other objects, repeating and absorbing the English words. For nearly an hour she asked the names of various items within sight. She may have abandoned her home and left her formal education behind, but her thirst for knowledge had never left her. Pistol, sword, saddle, skirt, blouse, horse, boots. The English words sounded strange, but she stored them up.

Finally, she yawned. It had been another long day in the saddle. Her yawn was infectious, and Alder yawned, too. Bella stretched out, resting her head on Gabby's saddle. She pulled her waist-length jacket closer around her. The night was chilly in the mountains. She watched warily as Alder stood and approached her holding a blanket. Her hand grasped the butt of one of her pistols, concerned that he might try to do something to her. He saw her not so subtle move and flashed a friendly, lopsided grin. He handed her the blanket, a spare one, and then backed away.

"*Gracias?*" Bella said, posing it as a question.

"Thank you," he replied.

"Thank you, Alder." Bella was grateful for the added warmth of the blanket. It smelled of sweaty horse, but no more so than the saddle blanket she lay on. She soon fell asleep, still clutching her pistol underneath the blanket.

Alder sat for a while captivated by Bella's lovely face, staring at her in the light of the dying fire. I don't know where she's going, he thought, but wherever it is, I'm going there, too, if she'll have me.

Bella awoke at first light to find Alder hunched by the fire, stoking the embers back to flame. His back was to her, and she watched as he heated water to make tea. He was stirring something in the pot he had used to cook beans the night before. He turned, and seeing that she was awake, gave her a friendly smile. "Good morning, Miss Bella."

"Good morning, Alder," she parroted back. She threw back the blanket and sat up. She had slept peacefully and unmolested all night. Needing to answer the call of nature, Bella stood and walked a little distance away to find privacy in a copse of stunted cottonwoods. As she returned to camp, she came upon a large rattlesnake coiled directly in her path, rattling its tail with the distinctive sound that once heard was never forgotten. Bella recalled being thrown from her pony when she encountered a rattler at the age of eight. She drew her pistol and shot the snake through the head.

A moment later, Alder came on the run to see what was the matter. He clutched a pistol in his right hand, and a wooden spoon in his left. He saw Bella, smoke curling from the muzzle of her pistol, and a rattler, a dozen feet from her with its head completely blown off. She knows how to shoot, he thought, gaining an added measure of respect for the young girl on her own in the wilderness.

"Rattlesnake," he said, pointing toward the serpent. "Good to eat."

Bella repeated, "Rattlesnake," but did not understand the rest of what he said. She got it, however, when Alder picked up the six-foot-long snake and carried it back to camp. She watched as he sliced open the snake's underbelly and removed its entrails. He expertly skinned the snake and set it to roast over the fire, skewered on a sharpened stick, meat for breakfast to supplement the porridge he was cooking in the pot.

The snake roasted quickly, and Alder put a slab of it on the tin plate, along with a glop of porridge for Bella. He poured her a tin cup of tea. She was not a tea drinker, preferring the dark smoky coffee she had enjoyed every day at home. Father Diaz had sometimes drunk tea, especially if he was feeling under the weather, and Bella had tried it a few times with him. Still, she was grateful for a warm drink on a chilly morning. The porridge was gluey, and she was reluctant to eat snake until she tried it. Then she understood what Alder meant by, "Good to eat." It was a little like chicken, and a lot not like chicken, but delicious, nevertheless. She was beginning to warm to this American who had fed her dinner and breakfast.

After breaking camp came the moment of truth. With pointing and gestures Alder asked Bella which way she was headed. "*Norte*," Bella replied, pointing in that direction. Alder had been headed south, thinking he might pass through Mexico and end up in South America. Change of plans.

He indicated that he, too, was traveling north, back the way he had come. He made it clear that he wanted to travel with her, and after giving it a moment's thought, Bella nodded her head. She was starting to believe she could trust him. It was only the two of them, together out in the wilds of the Sierra Madre. Had he intended to take advantage of her, he could easily have done so while she was sleeping.

They saddled up and headed out, Bella on her dappled gray mare, and Alder on a roan gelding. As they rode side-by-side, Bella pointed out plants, lizards, birds, and landmarks, and Alder told her their English names, at least the ones he knew. Bella would repeat the names to herself, and retained them. Alder also gave her verbs to go with her nouns: riding, flying, walking, sitting, standing. She was eager to learn this strange-sounding language. A notion popped into her head that one day being fluent in English might be valuable. Perhaps one day, when the war between the English and Americans ended, she might venture to a brand new country, for a brand new start, if that is, the Americans won their struggle for freedom. She knew the British colonies in America were a long way off, but really had no understanding of just how far away they were. She did not know it had taken Alder nearly a year to travel from the mountains of Pennsylvania to the Sierra Madre of Old Mexico.

They stopped at a stream midday to rest, and the English lessons continued. They watered the horses, refilled canteens, and ate what was left over of the breakfast snake meat. As they rode on, they came upon a dry wash where half a dozen grunting javelina, also known as collared peccaries, were rooting among the cacti. Alder reined in his horse and started to slowly draw his musket from its saddle scabbard. Bella immediately saw what he intended, drew her two pistols, and fired two shots. One of the small, wild pigs, about eighty feet away, dropped as though it had been poleaxed. Alder turned in his saddle to stare at her in amazement.

"That was some fine pistol shooting, Miss Bella."

From his broad grin, she caught his drift even if the only words she understood were 'pistol' and her name. The rest of the javalina herd scattered, and even though there was plenty of daylight left, Bella and Alder decided to make camp there for the night. They dismounted and tethered the horses. While Alder went to work with his knife skinning and dressing out the seventy pound pig, Bella began gathering fire wood. They would dine on roast pork that evening.

Some of the meat was hung on sticks to dry, but a roasted haunch, served with more beans, was delicious. Bella would have had no idea how to prepare game for cooking, but she paid close attention to what Alder was doing. It was messy and bloody, but there was plenty enough meat on the small porker to last them a number of days. She also discovered that soaking the beans before cooking tenderized them.

That evening, after eating, Alder moved his saddle closer to hers. They lay with their heads on the saddles facing each other, five feet apart. "Goodnight," Alder said, and Bella repeated it back to him. She drifted into sleep with a smile on her face.

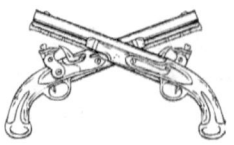

CHAPTER SEVENTEEN

For the next two weeks, Bella and Alder continued traveling north, meandering through the Sierra Madre. They rode side-by-side whenever possible, conversing in English. Bella's broken English became less broken with each passing day. At night they slept next to each other, only a foot or two apart. The only other people they encountered were a few scattered prospectors looking for elusive gold, and the occasional isolated farm family trying to scratch a living out of rocky soil.

One night before going to sleep, Alder moved closer to Bella, whispered the word "kiss," and followed up with a demonstration. It was her first proper kiss, not some quick peck on the forehead or cheek by her uncle or grandfather, and only the once by Julio, the day she fled her home. By then she had come to trust Alder completely. He laid his rough hand against her smooth cheek and tenderly kissed her soft lips.

"Kiss," Bella repeated to retain the word, but also because she wanted more of feeling his lips pressed against hers. He kissed her eagerly, hungrily, and she responded. That night they only kissed, but Bella slept spooned in his arms, and had never felt more secure.

Finally clearing the mountains, they came into a town. Alder had passed through there on his way south, and he knew there was a cantina that served food and had rooms for the night. Bella and Alder stabled their horses in a ramshackle barn behind the cantina and rented a room. Bella paid for the room and dinner with silver pesos. She had yet to use her seven large gold coins. Alder was not even aware that Bella was carrying that much money, a small fortune by his standards.

There was a bathroom with a bathtub, and Bella was able to bathe for the first time in weeks. A woodfired stove sat in the corner to heat wooden buckets of water. The tub was not particularly clean, and there was no scented soap, or any soap at all, for that matter, but it felt like the lap of luxury to soak the dirt and dust away. She pounded her split skirt against a wall to dislodge as much grit as she could. She had clean undergarments and a clean blouse in her satchel. She returned to the room where Alder was waiting. There was only one bed, and Bella stared at it a long time, wondering what might happen later that night.

Alder returned from washing up, and together they went down to the main room and ordered beef and beans for dinner, the only fare offered. They washed down the food with glasses of beer.

Finally, it was time to go back to the room. More patrons had drifted into the cantina, mostly rough-looking characters. The majority of the customers were men, but there were a few hard-case women as well. Many of the men were giving Bella the eye, so it seemed safer to retreat upstairs. There was a feeling of awkwardness between Bella and Alder as he shut and locked the door. They stood silently looking at each other for a long time. Finally Bella untied her blouse and pulled it off over her head. Underneath she wore a lace-trimmed chemise. She shed her skirt, and stood shivering nervously in only her chemise and pantaloons. Alder feasted his eyes on her shapely body, looking her over from head to feet. She was more lovely, more desirable than he had even imagined. He extended his arms and she went to him. They kissed, long and passionately. Finally Alder took her by the hand and led her to the bed. That night Bella gave herself to him, and slept wrapped securely in his arms.

Early in the morning, while Bella still slept, Alder rose from the bed, dressed, and went downstairs to find food to take back to the room. The cantina's kitchen was closed, so he ventured into the street to see what he could find. There was a bodega a little way down from the cantina that also served as a post office, with a jail cell out back. It, too, was closed, but as Alder stepped onto the wooden walkway in front of the store to peer through the window, he froze. There was a wanted poster nailed to the outside wall of the building. The drawing of Bella was crude, but he did not have to read Spanish to make out her name: Isabella Vasquez, and below her picture: 200 Pesos.

Alder snatched the poster off the wall and hurried back to the room. Bella awoke when he opened the door. She smiled, stretched, and extended her arms, inviting him to return to bed. He showed her the poster, and her smile vanished in an instant. Two hundred silver pesos, dead or alive. The bounty on her head had been doubled.

"Get dressed. We have to go right now," he said urgently. He had no idea why she was wanted, only that the young woman he loved had a price on her head.

Bella did not have to understand every word to know what he was saying. Immediately she threw aside the bedcovers and swung her legs out of bed. In two minutes she had put on her blouse, skirt and jacket, and slipped her feet into her boots. She tied the sash around her waist, stuck her pistols through the sash, and attached her rapier. Alder gathered up the rest of their things, and they hurried downstairs.

They left the cantina by the front door, but as they came around the side of the building headed for the barn, they encountered a party of seven men lying in wait. Bella had been seen in the main room of the cantina the night before, and the men wanted the reward. The poster explained why she had been stared at so intently. It was not only her beauty that drew these men's attention, but the price on her head as well.

The men were a motley collection of gauchos, farmers, and hired hands. They carried a hodgepodge collection of weapons. Two were armed with ancient muskets, and two more with pistols. One had a sword, and the final two carried only knives. Alder had two pistols—Bella had given him one she had taken from her first pursuers – and she was armed with her two guns.

The men did not look as though they were interested in the alive part of the offer when dead would do. The men with the muskets were already aiming their guns at Bella and Alder before they had a chance to draw their weapons. Alder raised his hands in a gesture of surrender. Bella hesitated, her hands moving toward her guns.

"No, Bella!" Alder said, knowing the muskets would cut her down before she could draw her pistols, no matter how fast she was.

Suddenly a shot rang out, and Bella flinched, certain the shot had been meant for her, until she saw one of the men with a musket crumple and fall to the ground. A second shot quickly followed, and Bella looking to her right, saw the grandest sight she could have imagined. Julio Higuera, mounted on a big bay gelding, was holding a smoking pistol in each hand. Next to Julio, astride a smaller black and white paint mare, sat Sesasi.

The two men with the pistols turned toward Julio, but Bella jerked her pistols from the sash and cut both men down before they could fire. The man with the sword charged Bella. It was she who had the price on her head. Bella drew her rapier and in short order disarmed her opponent, who immediately turned tail and fled, as did the two men armed with knives when Alder drew his pistols.

Alder had no idea what was going on, why this grizzled old timer would come to their aid, and he was even more surprised when the man dismounted, and Bella rushed to him, throwing herself into his waiting arms.

"Julio, you found me, you found me," Bella cried gleefully. "How ...?"

"My Bellita, we will talk later. Quickly, get your horse. We must flee now."

Bella turned to Sesasi and grinned from ear-to-ear, delighted to see the Indian woman, her beloved former nanny.

Bella then spoke to Alder in broken English, "John, we go." She hurried into the barn, with Alder right behind her. In minutes they had their horses saddled and bridled, and rode out of the barn. Julio had reloaded his pistols while Bella and the man with her were getting their horses. Bella's guns had been fired, but she still had spare loaded pistols in her satchel.

Already knots of armed men on foot were gathering in the center of the road at either end of town. "What do we do?" Bella asked Julio.

"We charge," he replied, and put his spurs to his horse's flanks. Bella followed suit, with Alder at her left side, and Sesasi at her right. Guiding their horses with their knees, brandishing pistols in both hands, Bella's party charged down the dusty road at a full gallop. Men raised weapons, but Bella, Alder, and Julio fired their guns. Two men fell, and the others scattered as the horses thundered down on them.

Two wild shots rang out behind them as Bella and the others raced out of town, but no one was hit. The party continued at a full gallop across a flat plain until the horses were panting with exhaustion. Finally Julio signaled for everyone to halt to give the horses a rest. Everyone dismounted and walked the horses into a deep draw that had a small watering hole in the shade of a stand of cottonwoods. As the horses drank their fill, Bella made introductions, and again hugged Julio and then Sesasi.

"This is my American friend, John Alder," Bella said, taking Alder's hand in hers. "Alder, my friends, Julio Higuera and Sesasi."

Julio saw the way Bella looked at Alder, and he at her, and he knew in that moment that Alder was more than merely her friend. His Bellita was no longer a girl, but now a woman.

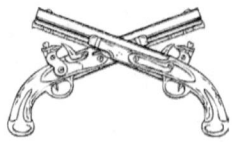

Chapter Eighteen

"When I learned there was a price on your head, I knew I had to find you," Julio told Bella that evening as they sat side-by-side at the campfire. Bella was delighted beyond words that Julio and Sesasi had joined her. The party was camped in a hidden gully, and Sesasi, having taken over cooking duties from Alder, was preparing dinner. Alder sat across from Bella, watching her converse with the old man in Spanish. She had explained to him the best she could in broken English who Julio and Sesasi were. Just as he was teaching Bella English, he had picked up a little Spanish from her, but she and Julio were talking way to fast for Alder to understand more than a few scattered words and phrases.

"Julio, I have killed so many men," Bella bemoaned. Tears welled up in her eyes at the thought. She related the incident inside the cantina in the first dusty little village, shooting the man who had grabbed her and the barman when he pointed the shotgun at her. Then there were the three riders who came after her seeking the reward. She had killed one of those men and wounded two others. "Those men may have died."

"They did not," Julio assured her. "Sesasi and I passed through their village. Those men were alive. I spoke with the one you stabbed in the shoulder. He told me you bandaged their wounds and helped them onto their horses. Because of those men Sesasi and I knew we were on your right trail. I am very proud of you, Bellita. May I continue to call you that?"

"Of course. I like that you call me your little Bella. But Julio, how can you be proud of me? I shot two more men today, and I do not know if I killed them. I am a murderer, Julio."

"No, you are not. Do not think that. In each case you were defending yourself. A murderer is a coward, one who lies in wait, one who takes a life for money, or revenge, or some other evil motive. Bellita, those men in the cantina, they might have done bad things to you. They might have done bad things and then killed you afterward to cover their crime. You had every right to defend yourself. The same today, and with those men who chased after you. The price on your head is unjust. You have done nothing wrong."

"It feels as though I have done everything wrong. Leaving home was wrong."

"No, it was not. If you had stayed and married that pompous dandy, Francisco, you would have been miserable for the rest of your life. If there is blame here, it falls on the shoulders of your father, the Don. I have watched you grow from a little girl into a fine young woman. Your father should have loved and cherished you. He did not. You are a rare jewel, Bellita. Your father should have protected you from men like Francisco, not tried to force you into marriage with someone like him. He did it for his own gain, putting his desires ahead of the welfare of his beautiful daughter. If you were my daughter, I would give my life to protect you."

Julio put his arm around Bella's shoulders and pulling her close, kissed the side of her head.

"I am afraid you have put *your* life in danger now," Bella said. "You shot men today. There will be a price on your head, too."

"That does not worry me. I was a soldier. I was never afraid in battle, well, perhaps a little, but my greatest fear is something happening to you. If you will have my company, I will stay with you and protect you until the end of my days."

"Of course I want you to stay with me. You left my father's employ? How is it you brought Sesasi with you?"

"When word reached your father's hacienda that there was a price on his daughter's head, as I told you, I knew I had to try to find you. I told the Don there must be a terrible mistake. I lied to him, and told him I would find you and bring you back safely so everything could be made right. When Sesasi heard that I was going in search of you, she insisted on coming with me. We packed plenty of provisions because we knew we would not be going back there. Life on your father's hacienda is now dead to us. We will stay with you, Bellita."

Bella kissed his bristly cheek. "I love you and Sesasi, Julio. Thank you for teaching me how to use a sword, and how to shoot."

"We love you, too, and it was my pleasure to be your teacher. No man has ever had a finer pupil. You have far surpassed this old sergeant's ability."

"Thank you for saving our lives today. I was certain I would be shot or hanged."

"Bellita, you do not need to thank me for rescuing you. I would die if something bad happened to you." Julio nodded at Alder sitting across the fire watching them. "What of that man? You have had relations with him? I only ask. I do not judge you. Do you love him?"

"Yes. I mean we had relations, but only once. I do not know if I love him. I like him. He has been kind to me. He teaches me English."

Alder felt like an outsider. Bella, Julio and Sesasi, were speaking to each other in rapid-fire Spanish, and he could not understand what there were saying. He realized they were old friends, but did not know exactly what the relationship between them was. Bella seemed particularly attached to the old man, Julio, and the Indian woman was clearly devoted to Bella, serving her dinner first, making sure Bella was comfortable, and generally fussing over her. Truthfully, he was jealous of the attention being lavished on Bella, and particularly so by Julio. Clearly he was not her father. She had introduced him as a friend. Was he a rival for her affections? Was it possible that the man, more than old enough to be Bella's father, was really a former lover? Bella was so young, and Julio was so very old, and yet he freely kissed her on her forehead, and on her cheek, and she returned his kisses in a similar manner. He began to think he ought to take his leave in the morning and continue with his original plans, travel south, perhaps all the way to South America.

That night, however, as everyone was settling down to sleep, Bella brought her blanket to where Alder was lying and lay down close beside him. She kissed him sweetly and tenderly, and a slow smile spread across his face. He enfolded her in his arms, and kissed her back eagerly. No, he thought, I will not leave this girl. I love her and I will stay with her as long as she will have me. She will learn English, and I will learn Spanish, and we will stay together no matter what. Where she goes, I will go.

Sharing a blanket, they again quietly made love once Julio was snoring loudly on the opposite side of the fire. Sesasi, also sleeping, was snuggled under a blanket with Julio. Bella fell asleep with her head pillowed on Alder's shoulder. He lay awake for a while, his nose buried in the mass of Bella's dark curls.

No men from the village pursued them. Evidently the number of men cut down in the showdown at the barn, and in the wild escape from the town, had convinced the townsmen that it was not worth the risk, even for two hundred silver pesos, to tangle with the newly notorious bandit, Isabella Vasquez, and her gang.

As for Bella, she had no idea that she was considered a dangerous bandit. Julio's speech of the previous night, a lot of words for a normally taciturn man, had convinced her that she was not a murderer, that she had only done what she needed to do to defend herself. All Bella wanted was to get away, go north across the Rio Grande, and hopefully start a new and peaceful life there. When she shared her plans with Julio, he heartily agreed that it was a good one. He knew there were Spanish outposts in the territory north of the border river, a fort in the village of Tucson, in the southern part of the Arizona Territory, and the old, well-established city of Santa Fe in northern New Mexico, but most of the country was wide open land.

Julio was worried, however, because much of that wild desert was peopled with war-like Indians, particularly the Apache, who occasionally raided across the river to steal cattle. He knew this from a brief stint on border patrol duty while a private in the army, long before joining Captain Domingo Vasquez' company in the South. Still, with a price on Bella's head, and now probably on his as well, going north and leaving Old Mexico seemed like the only viable option. Perhaps, Julio thought, Bella's American friend Alder might be of some use in the land across the Rio Grande.

Bella's party set out early the next morning, and traveled for two weeks with no sign of pursuit. Late one afternoon, they came to the edge of a bluff, and looking down, saw below them the broad Rio Grande. They had made it to the border.

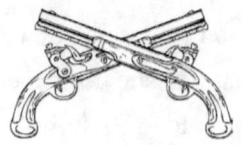

Chapter Nineteen

After camping for the night atop the bluff on the Old Mexico side of the river, Bella and her party descended a narrow trail to the river bank. Trusting the horses to swim, they rode into the green water. The current was swift, and the river deep at that time of year. Rainfall in mountains too distant to see filled streams and creeks that flowed south into the Rio Grande. The horses struggled, and Gabby stumbled on a slippery rock as they approached the north bank. Bella fought to remain in the saddle, but was thrown off as Gabby struggled to regain her footing.

Bella went into the water, flailing wildly, and crying out for help. She had never learned how to swim and was being swept downstream. Alder was off his horse in a flash, diving headlong into the river. He swam with powerful strokes, determined that Bella was not going to drown. As a boy, he had grown up on a farm near a small lake and had swum there nearly every summer day. Alder caught up to Bella and grabbed her around the waist. She flung her arms around his neck, clinging to him so tightly he found it difficult to breathe. He stood, swooping Bella up in his arms. To her embarrassment, the water only came up to his waist that close to the river bank. She realized that had she not been in such a panic, she could have gotten her footing and waded to shore.

Alder set Bella on her feet, and she kissed him passionately. "You must learn how to swim," he said. She did not know every word, but understood what he was telling her. Julio and Sesasi rode up leading the other two horses. Bella and Alder were completely soaked, and Julio and Sesasi were wet from the waist down. All of the pistols needed to be cleaned and reloaded, and clothing had to be dried. Sesasi began gathering firewood, while Bella and Alder stripped to their under garments. They huddled together under a blanket close to the fire Julio built. Their wet clothing was hung on nearby tree branches to dry. Cold and wet, at least they were alive, uninjured, and had made it across the river.

It was late morning when Bella deemed her skirt, blouse and jacket were dry enough to put on. The fire had warmed her, but it was the hot desert sun that did most of the drying. Alder had already put on his pants and jacket, and was helping Julio dry, clean, and reload the guns. He cleaned Bella's fancy dueling pistols first, and was surprised to discover the bores were rifled, highly unusual for pistols. The markings on the guns indicated they were of English make. No wonder she is such a fine shot with these, he thought. Most pistols, and muskets were smoothbores. The lack of rifling made guns easier and faster to load, but accuracy suffered. Rifling put a spin on the bullet that stabilized it. He had witnessed Bella take down a javalina from a distance that would be a stretch with a musket.

Alder had an appreciation for fine guns. As a boy, he had hunted in the fields and woods around his family's farm with a slim, small caliber Pennsylvania rifle. He brought home a lot of rabbits and squirrels with that gun, putting needed meat on the table. He reloaded and re-primed the pistols and returned them to Bella.

She had just tucked the pistols away in her sash when suddenly three Indians silently appeared out of the brush at the edge of the campsite. Immediately she started to reach for her guns, but Julio, standing nearby, stayed her hands. Warily he approached the three Natives, his hand held up in greeting, and addressed them in Spanish. They were too far away for Bella to make out the conversation, but it was clear that the Indians understood and responded to what Julio was discussing with them.

While Julio talked, Bella studied the three native men. Unlike the Indians in Old Mexico, who were beaten down by over two hundred years of Spanish occupation and rule, virtual slaves, these men seemed proud, standing straight and tall. They were of differing ages. The oldest wore his gray hair in two long braids hanging over his shoulders. His pants were made of buckskin, but he wore a shirt of woven cloth. The second man was taller, the tallest of the three, with jet black hair worn loose, but tied back with a cloth band around his forehead. He was dressed completely in buckskin. The youngest, little more than a boy, wore his black hair in a single braid and was clad in both cloth pants and shirt. The two older men carried Spanish muskets; the boy was unarmed except for a hunting knife.

Fascinated, Bella wanted a closer look at these Native Americans. She went to Julio's side, and he introduced her to the men, and her to them. It turned out that they were of the Chiricahua Apache tribe, three generations of the same family, grandfather, father, and son. They were hunting, and having seen the smoke from the campfire, came to investigate. They spoke broken Spanish, picked up at a distant trading post. The grandfather's name was Kuruk, which he said meant Bear. The father was Nitis, Friend, and the son was Tarak, or Star.

The three Native American men looked Bella over, taking note of her pistols and the rapier dangling from her hip. A faint smile played across Kuruk's face. He nodded at Bella and said, "Dahteste."

Bella did not understand, but Julio laughingly said, "That's quite an honor. I believe you've just been given an Apache name."

Bella arched her graceful eyebrows in surprise. She repeated, "Dahteste. What does that mean?" she asked, directing her question to Kuruk.

"You are Warrior Woman."

That made Bella smile. *Warrior Woman, is that how I am seen? Is that what I have become.* She extended her hand, and Kuruk, having witnessed deals at the trading post being made on a handshake, took her hand in his. Kuruk invited Bella and her party to return to the Apache camp with him and his son and grandson. Bella readily agreed, desiring to learn more about these proud, free people.

Julio concurred. "They seem friendly enough. If they meant us harm, they would have attacked us from ambush," he told Bella in an aside as they went back to put out the fire and gather their horses.

Bella, in her broken English, explained to Alder what was happening, "Apache Indian. We go they camp."

"Their camp," he automatically corrected her, and Bella nodded, not minding the correction, but rather welcoming it. She wanted badly to learn proper English.

Alder was dismayed that the party was going with three strange Apache Indians to their encampment, where there would be many more Apaches. His experiences with Native Americans had always been unpleasant. As a boy, Huron raiders had from time-to-time terrorized the frontier where his family's farm was located. Their farm had been spared, but neighboring families, men, women, and children had been wiped out, slaughtered mercilessly, their homes and barns burned to the ground. His own uncle and aunt had suffered such a fate farther upcountry from the Alder farm.

When he traveled across Tejas, or Texas as some called it, and New Mexico, he had been careful to avoid encounters with Indians. The fierce Comanche had a reputation for raiding far and wide throughout the Southwest, and Alder had heard tales of the ferocious fighting ability of the Apache, sworn enemies of the Comanche. Now Bella was determined to visit these Indians in their camp? What choice did he have? He would not abandon the beautiful girl with whom he had fallen deeply in love, and there was no changing her stubborn mind. He saddled his horse, and with the others, followed the three Apaches to a stand of cottonwoods where their horses were tethered. A dead Pronghorn antelope—really a distant member of the sheep family—lay across the rump of one of the Apache horses.

It was a ride of many miles inland away from the river to reach the Apache encampment. For most of the ride the party was strung out single file following twisting game trails, climbing higher into cactus covered hills. They emerged onto a broad plateau late in the afternoon, and the first thing Bella noticed was a score or more of wickiups, the Southwest Indians equivalent of the teepee. The rounded huts were framed with wood and covered in animal hides, easy to set up and to take down, as the nomadic tribe moved, following migrating game.

Smoke curled up through openings in the centers of the domed tops of the wickiups. Children were running and shouting throughout the camp, chasing each other, playing games. Dogs barked as the riders entered the camp, and women hard at work preparing the evening meal, stopped to stare at the four strangers accompanying the hunters. Most of their attention was focused on Bella. It was not that unusual to see Spanish traders riding in groups throughout the Southwest, but the sight of a young Spanish lady, and especially one heavily armed, was a rare sight indeed.

Kuruk led Bella and the others to his wickiup where an older woman was preparing corn cakes in a cast iron skillet over an open outdoor fire. His son, Nitis, unloaded the carcass of the Pronghorn from the back of his horse. The animal had already been field dressed, and he set to work skinning and quartering it.

Bella and the others were shown where to tether their horses. They left their saddles on the ground nearby. The Apache had no need of saddles; they rode bareback. Bella and the others rejoined Kuruk who was sitting by the fire. He introduced Bella as Dahteste to his wife Gouyen, which he explained meant Wise Woman. That made Bella smile. Gouyen, clad in a buckskin tunic, had a serious, no-nonsense look of wisdom about her. Like her husband, her gray hair was braided in twin braids, but long, falling to her waist. Bella watched as the woman fried corn cakes filled with bits of shredded meat, seeds, and berries in animal fat. When done, she would lift the cakes out of the skillet with a hand-carved wooden spatula and set them on a wooden rack to cool while she started another batch. She silently handed Bella, Julio, Alder, and Sesasi each a cooled cake. Bella thought they were delicious. Sesasi offered to help with the cooking, but was rebuffed when Gouyen grunted in broken Spanish that she was a guest.

Soon a rear quarter of the pronghorn was spitted and roasting over the fire. The rest of the animal had been shared with other families in the tribe. Children gathered to stare at the strangers, and Bella noticed one little girl wearing a buckskin tunic standing a little closer than the others, shyly staring at her. She motioned for the child to join her. The little girl, around five or six, hesitated, but then approached Bella. She gave the child half of her corn cake and patted the ground next to her, indicating for the girl to sit. Staring up at Bella with big brown eyes, the girl sat close by Bella's side, and Bella put her arm around the child. Bella had grown up without siblings or other children as friends. The young Apache girl fascinated her.

"My name is Bella." The girl just stared, so Bella pointed to herself and repeated, "Bella."

The little girl got it, and pointing to herself, said, "Nascha."

Kuruk, watching the interaction from across the fire, said, "She is Little Owl, Nitis' daughter, my granddaughter. Only I and a few others speak much Spanish."

"She is a beautiful child. Thank you, Kuruk, for your hospitality."

"You are most welcome, Dahteste," Kuruk replied.

"I appreciate the name you gave me, but I am not really a warrior woman," Bella said, laughing.

"I believe you are, or you will be one day. You lead, and your friends follow. Among my people, we have had many women warriors. Apache women fight to protect their families. You have killed. I see it in your eyes."

Bella sat silently stunned. How could this old Indian man see into her soul through the window of her eyes? The fact that she had killed three men for certain, and possibly three or four others, ate away at her. All had been in self-defense, but that did not change the fact that men once alive and breathing were now dead at her hands.

Bella excused herself for a moment, stood, and retrieved her battered leather satchel. Sitting back down next to Nascha, she open the satchel and removed the velvet pouch containing the rosary she had received from her grandfather for her First Communion. She drew the rosary out of its pouch, and holding it in her hand, showed it to the little girl.

At home Bella had prayed the rosary on her knees at the side of her bed every night before crawling under the covers to sleep. The first couple of nights on her own, before the ill-fated incident in the cantina, she had taken comfort in repeating the strings of Our Fathers and Hail Marys while lying by the camp fire. After killing the two men in the cantina, however, she felt guilty, and believed it would be hypocritical to pray after taking those lives. She had thought of herself as a murderer, and without a priest to hear her confession, was damned if she died. She had not prayed the rosary since.

Bella placed the rosary around Nascha's neck. "For you," she told the little girl. The child's eyes lit up with delight, and fascinated, she fingered the smooth ivory beads and the gold crucifix for the rest of the evening.

Bella and her friends feasted with Kuruk and his family, and throughout the evening other members of the tribe came by Kuruk's camp fire to see the strangers, and to join in chanting Apache songs. Bella could not understand the words, but found the unfamiliar cadences oddly soothing.

It was late when she and Alder crawled under a blanket together next to the campfire. Kuruk had invited her to sleep inside the wickiup, but it was a beautiful night, and Bella preferred to be outdoors, sleeping with her lover under the star-filled sky. Julio and Sesasi again shared a blanket on the opposite side of the fire.

CHAPTER TWENTY

In the morning, Bella and her companions were again fed corn cakes for breakfast before taking their leave. In gratitude for Kuruk's hospitality, she gave him one of the pistols she had taken from her pursuers along with a supply of gunpowder and lead pistol balls. She had told her Indian host that her intention was to travel to the town of Santa Fe in the New Mexico Territory. Santa Fe was the second oldest city in North America after Saint Petersburg in the Spanish territory of Florida.

"That is a long journey, Dahteste," Kuruk told her. "You must beware of Comanche raiders. The Comanche will kill you for your horses. They are mad for horses and never satisfied with what they have."

Bella thanked him for the warning and saddled Gabby while Alder, Julio, and Sesasi readied their mounts. They said goodbye to their new Apache friends and headed out, riding north by east, following a well-worn trail through patches of cacti and sagebrush. They were descending from the plateau when Alder, riding beside Bella, spotted a dust cloud in the distance. In his saddlebag he had a small brass spyglass that had belonged to the British dispatch rider he had killed. After he extended it and looked, he turned to Bella and said, "Comanche war party."

"How many?"

He looked again for a minute. "I count twenty." He hesitated a moment and added, "It looks like they're headed for the Apache camp we just left."

Bella blanched. Kuruk and his family, and the other Apaches who had welcomed them and fed them, little Nascha, they were all at risk of being slaughtered by the blood-thirsty Comanche. "We go back. We help them," Bella said in broken English.

"What?" Alder asked alarmed. "It's none of our business. The Comanche and Apache have been enemies for generations. Besides there are only four of us."

Bella only understood about half of what he said, but from his tone she could tell he was against aiding their Apache hosts. She turned to Julio, and pleaded, "We have to help Kuruk."

He stared at the girl who was like a daughter to him, and thought to himself, she does have the heart of a warrior. Dahteste is a good name for my Bellita. He nodded his head. "Friends help friends. We can come down on their flank and surprise them."

Bella turned to Alder and said in English, "You stay here," and then to Sesasi in Spanish, "You stay with Alder. Julio and I will go."

"No," Alder replied. If you go, I go."

Sesasi said, "Give me a pistol, I will not stay behind."

Bella made sure her spare pistols were loaded and primed and gave one to Sesasi, and another to Alder. They turned their horses and followed the Comanche dust trail back in the direction from which they had just come. They arrived at the Apache camp while it was under attack. The Comanche had the reputation of being among the finest horsemen anywhere. Very few were armed with muskets, which were difficult to wield from horseback. They much preferred their short bows which were far easier to use from the back of a galloping horse than a long gun, and far quicker to reload with a fresh arrow.

As Bella and her party arrived, she saw several of the wickiups in flames. The Apache were fighting back, with Spanish muskets, but also with bows. Several of the Comanche were trying to steal the Apache horses. There was shouting, and screaming, and gunfire. Smoke choked the air. It was chaos. There were men and women, dead or wounded, on the ground, some Comanche warriors, but most of the dead and injured were members of the Apache tribe.

Bella spotted Kuruk aiming the pistol she had given him at a mounted Comanche raider charging down on him wielding a lance. Kuruk fired and the Comanche tumbled from his horse. Bella pulled out her two pistols and charged into the fray, flanked by Alder and Julio, with Sesasi right behind. Bella fired, once, twice, felling two Comanche warriors. She shoved the pistols back into her sash and drew her rapier. Alder shot one Comanche and missed one. Julio downed two more with his pistols, and then, like Bella, drew his sword.

The Comanche, taken by surprise from behind, were thrown into confusion. One warrior turned around and shot an arrow at Bella, narrowly missing her. Before he could fit another arrow to his bowstring, she put her heels to Gabby's flanks and charged the man. He was shocked to see a girl bearing down on him. He pulled out his tomahawk and came at her, taking a wide swing at her head. Bella dodged the blow and stabbed the warrior in the side with her sword. He remained on his horse, but fled, severely wounded.

Alder dismounted and aimed his musket at another Comanche, felling him at close range. With the Apache fighting back fiercely, and Bella's party surprising them from the rear, the remaining Comanche fled, whooping and shouting war cries. They managed to steal about half of the Apache horses as they escaped.

When Bella turned to look to make sure her friends were okay, she saw Sesasi looking pale, and then noticed a Comanche arrow protruding from her Indian nursemaid's thigh. Julio saw the arrow, too, and quickly dismounting, ran to Sesasi's side. He lifted her from her horse's back and carried her to a clear area to lay her down.

Kuruk walked across the camp, past dead and wounded members of both tribes, and stood before Bella as she alit from her saddle. There were tears in the old man's eyes, and at first Bella thought they were tears of gratitude that she and the others had returned to help, but as she looked deep into the man's eyes, she saw incomparable sadness there. Looking past his shoulder, Bella saw Gouyen, Kuruk's wife, lying face down in the dirt, a Comanche arrow protruding from her back. Overcome with emotion, Bella's eyes flooded with tears, too, and she embraced the old man, refusing to let him go. "I am so sorry, my friend," she said softly next to his ear.

"Thank you, Dahteste," Kuruk finally said, when they released each other. "You *are* Dahteste. You came back to help us."

Echoing Julio's earlier statement, she replied, "Friends help friends in need."

Alder approached and cautioned Bella, "We should reload our guns in case they return."

Bella caught "reload" and "guns," and nodded her head. She left Kuruk so he could tend to his dead wife and went to help Julio with Sesasi. There was a large blood stain on Sesasi's skirt, and more blood running down her leg.

Julio looked grim. "The arrow is embedded. It will do more damage to try to pull it out. It must be pushed through, then the shaft can be broken and pulled out."

Sesasi nodded that she understood what needed to be done. Bella retrieved what remained of her spare petticoat from her satchel to use as a bandage, while Julio gave Sesasi a thick piece of leather strap to bite down on. Sesasi tried to hold stoically still, but could not help letting out muffled shrieks as Julio pushed the arrowhead the rest of the way through her outer thigh. Bella, her arms around Sesasi's shoulders, held her tight. Once the flint arrowhead was through the back of Sesasi's thigh, Julio grabbed the bloody shaft between his two hands and snapped off the head. He then pulled the shaft back out of the Sesasi's leg.

Bella continued to hold Sesasi as Julio used a needle and black thread to stitch the wounds closed. He then wound strips of Bella's linen petticoat around Sesasi's leg. Only after Sesasi was bandaged and resting did Bella reload her pistols.

Bella and Julio helped the Apaches tend their wounded and bury their dead. Alder tethered the party's horses and then kept watch in case the Comanche returned. In addition to several wounded, the Apache had lost three men killed, two women dead, including Gouyen, and a child, a girl of eleven. The bodies were wrapped in blankets, carried outside the camp, and buried in shallow graves. Mournful songs were sung as rocks were mounded over the graves. The Apache were superstitious and believed the ghosts of the fallen would haunt the place where they died, and so near the end of the day, the tribe took down the wickiups, packed their wounded and belongings onto travois, and moved the camp two miles away.

Bella, Julio, Alder, and Sesasi remained with the tribe for three more days, helping their Apache friends relocate the camp. Sesasi, like the other wounded, was moved on a travois pulled by her horse. Bella and Alder rode out hunting to bring meat back to camp, and Alder shot a deer with his musket.

It was a sad parting when Bella and the others finally took their leave. Kuruk gave Bella a razor sharp hunting knife of Spanish make in a beaded sheath decorated with two eagle feathers. They hugged, and Bella was misty-eyed as she mounted Gabby. Julio lifted Sesasi onto her horse, and the party set out with Bella and Alder in the lead. Bella wondered whether she would ever see Kuruk again. She was very fond of the Apache elder, and she hoped he would be all right without his wife.

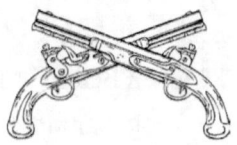

CHAPTER TWENTY-ONE

Bella's party resumed their journey north by east, taking their time, traveling slow because riding was painful for Sesasi. They kept a constant lookout for signs of hostile Indians. Kuruk had warned Bella that not only were the Comanche to be feared, but that not all Apache tribes were as friendly as his people. The Navajo, living father north, were relatively peaceful, but were unafraid to protect their vast tribal lands from invaders.

Bella and Alder hunted, and Bella had as much success with her pistols bringing down game as Alder did with his musket. They sought out sheltered places to camp at night, shielding their campfires as best they could so not to draw attention. Bella and Alder continued to sleep together, and Julio shared a blanket with Sesasi. As the days and weeks passed, Bella's English improved markedly. She very much wanted to become fluent in the language. Even Julio and Sesasi began picking up a little English just from listening to Bella and Alder converse. When they camped one afternoon by a small lake, really no more than a pond, Alder taught Bella how to swim. Bella's seventeenth birthday passed without notice. She had lost all track of the days since leaving home.

It was the summer of 1782 when Bella and her friends arrived in Santa Fe, or properly, La Villa Real de la Santa Fe de San Francisco de Asís, named after Saint Francis of Assisi. The town had been established in 1607 at the foot of the Sangre de Cristo mountains, and it was the capitol of the New Mexico Territory. The town was built around a broad central plaza, with narrow streets and a few broad avenues radiating outward from there. The Palace of the Governors was on the north side of the plaza, while the Cathedral Basilica of Saint Francis of Assisi occupied the east side. Shops and eateries faced the plaza, which was a gathering place for the residents.

Bella and the others rode into town late in the day. The city put Bella in mind of Mexico City, but on a much less grand scale. They found a cozy inn a block away from the plaza, and took two rooms. Bella paid for two weeks in advance with one of her gold coins, the first one she had spent on her thousand mile journey.

"So what do we do here?" Alder asked after stabling the horses in a barn behind the inn.

Bella shrugged. "We live. We find work. There is a school. We rode past it when we entered the city. Maybe I can be a teacher. Maybe we will find a small casa." She hesitated a moment. "Maybe you and I will marry."

Alder looked at her in surprise. They had been sleeping together, but had never discussed tying the knot. "Is that what you want?"

"I do not know. Maybe. Do you love me?"

"Yes, of course, I do. You are the smartest, bravest, most beautiful girl in the world. What about you? Do you love me?"

"I think so, yes," Bella replied, her cheeks taking on a fetching blush. She was not quite sure how to tell him that she thought she might be pregnant. She knew how it worked, making babies. Growing up on a rancho where horses and cattle were bred, she had seen animals coupling, but she had never discussed with her mother what to expect in pregnancy.

They spoke no more of possible marriage at that time. Everyone was hungry and dirty. Bella had noticed a bank as they entered the plaza. She needed a bath and a change of clothing, they all did. She took two more of her gold coins to the bank and exchanged them for silver pesos, much easier to spend. She stopped in a shop on the way back to the inn and bought an embroidered blouse. After bathing in a real bathtub with real soap, the four of them, Bella wearing her new blouse, went to the plaza and entered a cozy cantina for a dinner of shredded roast beef with chilis, beans, and tortillas. Sesasi's leg was mostly healed, and she walked with only a slight limp. They drank wine with their meal, and afterward strolled the plaza along with dozens of residents. Bella bought Sesasi a woolen dress from a shop catering to women, and new shirts for Alder and Julio from a vendor of men's attire. It was a pleasant evening, cool, but not uncomfortably so, and the setting sun made the mountains glow with varying shades of bright red, thus giving them their name, the Blood of Christ.

After they returned to the inn, Julio and Sesasi to their room, and Bella and Alder to theirs, Alder asked, "What you said earlier, do you really want to get married?"

Again Bella hesitated a minute, and then blurted out, "I think I am with a baby."

"What?" Alder asked in surprise.

"I think I carry your baby," Bella repeated. "For that reason, we should marry. A baby must have a mother and father."

Alder was silent a minute, looking at the girl, the young woman, he loved. "You're right. A baby should have a mother and father. I never thought I was the marrying kind, but then I never knew a girl like you before. Therefore, yes, if it's what you want, we'll marry."

Bella went to him and, putting her arms around his neck, kissed him eagerly. "I do not know if I am still Catholic, but there is a church at the plaza. We will ask a priest there to marry us."

Julio was surprised, and a little worried when he learned Bella and Alder planned to marry. He knew they had been together for weeks, but he still thought of Bella as the little girl he had helped raise. It was hard to keep in mind that she was a young woman now, capable of making her own decisions. He still had reservations about Alder. They had gotten along okay during weeks on the trail, but he could not shake the feeling that Alder was not good enough for his Bellita. In Julio's eyes, maybe no man was. Bella had not shared with anyone other than Alder that she might be pregnant, but Sesasi had her suspicions. Sesasi had taken care of Bella from infancy and knew her more intimately than even Bella's own mother.

The following day Bella, dragging Alder with her, walked to the Basilica of Saint Francis of Assisi. After agreeing to marry Bella, Alder was beginning to have second thoughts, especially about getting married by a priest in a Catholic Church. Alder was without religion, not having attended church since he was a young boy. He thought that if they were going to do this, he would rather get hitched before a justice of the peace, if there were such an official in Catholic Santa Fe.

Bella, too, was nervous and hesitated before entering the church. She had not attended Mass in three months and was weighed down with guilt over killing men, even if the killings were done in self-defense. Finally she worked up the gumption to open the heavy wooden door and step inside. The interior of the cathedral was cool and dimly lit. Candles burned in an alcove in front of a statue of the Blessed Virgin. Bella dipped her fingers in the Holy Water fount, made the sign of the cross, and facing the altar, genuflected. Sunlight pouring through stained glass windows painted colored patterns on the stone floor. It was all very familiar, and yet seemed strange at the same time.

A friar, a Franciscan, of course, entered the nave from a side entrance. He spotted Bella and Alder standing in the aisle near the front doors and detoured from his destination to see if he could be of help.

"Good morning, Señorita, I am Father Raul Perez. How may I help you?" he asked in Spanish.

"Good morning, Father, I am Isabella Vasquez. This man is John Alder. We would like to be married."

"I see." The priest looked at Alder, who appeared to be extremely uncomfortable and was hanging back a few paces. "And you, Señor?"

"He does not have much Spanish," Bella explained. She hesitated a moment, and then added, "Father, he is not Catholic."

"And you are, my child?"

"I...I was raised Catholic, but I have not been to Mass in several months."

"Should I hear your confession?"

Again Bella hesitated. I have killed, she thought. I have had relations outside of marriage. The number and gravity of her sins suddenly overwhelmed her, and her eyes flooded with tears. I cannot do this, she told herself. How could God forgive so many sins? How could He forgive one such as me?

The priest said, "Unless you are both Catholic, you cannot marry in the Church."

Bella nodded. It was in that moment she decided to abandon the Church forever. Alder would never convert. She could not bring herself to enter the dark confessional and tell her secret sins to this priest, not after speaking to him face-to-face without the anonymity provided inside the confessional by the screen between priest and penitent. "Thank you for your time, Father." Bella turned on her heels and walked out the church door, followed closely by Alder.

"What happened? What did he say?" Alder asked, as they walked back toward the inn. He had picked up only a smattering of Spanish from her, whereas her English was becoming fluent.

Bella shook her head. "It does not matter. We will not marry, not in the Church, not anywhere. Our baby does not need a piece of paper signed by a priest to make her ours."

"Her?" Alder asked, with a wry smile. "Are you sure the baby will be a girl?"

Bella shrugged. "I feel it will be."

As they approached the inn, they were met by an anxious Julio. "We must leave right away!" he told Bella in Spanish. "Look!" He showed her a wanted poster with the same crude drawing of her likeness and the words: "Isabella Vasquez, Wanted Dead or Alive." The reward had been upped to 500 silver pesos.

Bella blanched. "Will I be hunted the rest of my life?" she asked aloud.

"Sesasi is in the barn saddling the horses," Julio told them. "Quickly, gather your things. A troop of soldiers from Mexico arrived just this morning. They know you are in this area, They are putting up these posters everywhere."

It was a repeat of the situation at the cantina where Bella and Alder had spent their first night together, on the day when Julio and Sesasi found them. This time, however, it was not a ragged band of ranch hands and idlers seeking a reward, but a cadre of trained soldiers.

Bella and Alder hurried up to their room. Already drinkers and diners in the main room of the cantina were staring. Bella stuffed her belongings into her satchel while Alder quickly packed his saddlebags. She checked her pistols to make sure they were loaded and primed, and tucked them into her waist sash. She had left her weapons in the room before going to the church, never dreaming that her notoriety would have followed her as far as Santa Fe. She hung her rapier over her hip and was ready to go.

As Alder opened the door to their room, he saw an officer and three enlisted men at the bottom of the stairs talking to the innkeeper, who was pointing up the staircase. He closed and locked the door. "Quick, out the window," he said. Bella lifted the window and swung her legs through.

There was a balcony that ran along the front of the building. More soldiers were milling about in the street below. One glanced up as Alder exited the room through the open window.

"There!" the soldier cried in Spanish. Other soldiers fumbled with their cumbersome muskets as Bella made a dash for the end of the balcony. Shots rang out. Bella hopped over the railing and dropped to the ground at the side of the building, landing hard on her feet. She felt a sharp pain as she twisted her ankle. Nevertheless, she had her pistols out before the first soldiers rounded the side of the inn. She fired two shots and two soldiers fell. The others drew back momentarily.

Alder was instantly at her side, having jumped after her. "Go!" he hollered, pointing toward the stable. Julio and Sesasi were already mounted on their horses waiting behind the inn, and were holding the reins of Gabby and Alder's horse. Limping on her sore ankle, Bella hobbled toward her horse. More shots rang out behind her. She glanced over her shoulder, and froze. Alder was standing with his back to her, facing the soldiers charging around the corner of the building. The troopers were led by the lieutenant he had seen inside the cantina. Smoke was curling from Alder's pistols, and the officer fell face first to the ground. Several soldiers stopped, knelt, and fired a volley. Bella watched in horror as Alder staggered back a few steps and then fell, sprawled in the dirt, his arms and legs splayed.

Bella started to draw her sword, but Julio hollered, "Bella, No!" He drew his pistols and felled two more soldiers as Sesasi rode to Bella leading Gabby. "Hurry!" Sesasi shouted, stopping briefly so Bella could mount her horse. After hoisting herself onto the saddle, she paused for a moment, staring at her fallen lover. He had sacrificed himself for her.

"Quickly!" Julio cried, turning his horse and releasing the reins of Alder's.

"Come, there is nothing you can do," Sesasi urged, placing her hand on Bella's arm.

Feeling numb, but knowing that every second's delay endangered not only her own life, but Julio's and Sesasi's as well, Bella turned Gabby, and put her heels to the mare's flanks. More shot were fired, but to no effect; Bella and her companions were moving fast and putting distance between themselves and the troopers. As they galloped through narrow streets to the edge of town, Bella hollered to Julio, "Where to?"

"North, into the mountains!" he shouted back.

Part Three

OUTLAWS

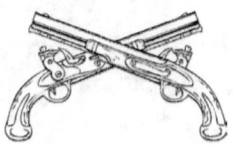

Chapter Twenty-Two

It did not take long for the army to assemble a mounted unit to pursue Bella, Julio, and Sesasi. The three companions rode hard, heading north into the Sangre de Cristo mountains. Julio thought Tejas, or Texas, would be a good ultimate destination. Texas was a vast territory, extending all the way to French Louisiana, and was sparsely populated, but the three companions needed to lose their pursuers first.

As soon as they began the climb along a narrow trail, they stopped and reloaded their guns. Bella's hands were trembling as she tried to load her pistols. Her cheeks were tear-streaked. She could not get the image of Alder lying dead on the ground out of her mind. Julio took the pistols from her after loading his own and finished loading and priming them.

"We were going to get married," Bella said quietly.

"I know, Bellita," Julio replied, placing his hand reassuringly on her shoulder. "He gave his life for you. I had reservations, but I misjudged him. I think he was a good man. Honor him by staying alive." He handed her back her pistols.

Julio had two muskets, his and Alder's, plus his pistols and sword. Sesasi still had the pistol Bella had given her when they rode to the aid of Kuruk and his tribe. They began moving again, climbing higher and higher up the winding trail.

Julio in the lead raised his hand indicating they should stop. With his trained military eye, he judged it was as good a place as any to make a stand. Behind them the trail was narrow, with a steep drop off to the left and towering cliffs to the right. The soldiers would have to come at them single file, and it would be almost impossible to be flanked. A jumble of large boulders, remnants of a past avalanche, provided good cover.

They dismounted and led the horses a little distance ahead, safely out of the line of fire. "Stay here with the horses," Julio told Sesasi, and then took the Indian woman in his arms and kissed her. "Bella and I will fight."

"I can help," Sesasi protested.

"You can be of most help by making sure the horses do not run off." Julio kissed her again, and then he and Bella headed back to the place they had picked for the ambush.

As they settled in to await their pursuers, Bella shook her head in disbelief. She was wanted and hunted. How had that happened? All she had wanted was to flee an arranged marriage to a man she loathed. All she desired was to be left alone, to lead a quiet life of her own choosing with a man she could love. "Will I be hunted the rest of my life?" she asked aloud. She was speaking rhetorically. She knew the answer.

Julio, believing she was addressing him, laid his hand on her arm. "Today we fight. We worry about tomorrow if we survive." He gave her a faint smile, hoping to appear confident. "They can only come at us one at a time, so we do not shoot together. I will fire the muskets, and then you will cover with your pistols while I reload. I hope these soldiers are not anxious to die."

"So much death," Bella bemoaned, but her resolution stiffened when she thought that it was probably some of these very soldiers who had gunned Alder down. I am an outlaw now, she told herself, and from now on an outlaw I will always be. Yes, Julio is right. The only way I can honor Alder is by staying alive and taking revenge on those who killed him.

Soon the first soldier appeared around the bend in the trail. It was a junior officer, and anticipating a possible ambush, he was moving cautiously. Julio drew a bead with a musket, not on the man in the lead, but on the soldier behind him. He fired, and that man tumbled from his horse, falling over the side of the cliff. The horse panicked, and tried to turn back, but other mounted soldiers were pressing forward and there was nowhere for the horse to go.

The officer at the head of the column reined in his horse, and Julio's second shot with the second musket dropped him. As Julio hunkered down to reload, Bella rested her pistols on the top of the rock that shielded her. Another soldier appeared and fell as her shot took him out of the saddle. There was confusion in the ranks of the soldiers. Some were pushing forward from behind, while others at the front tried to turn on the narrow trail to retreat from the deadly fire. Horses were screaming in panic, and one lost its footing and tumbled down the cliff. The dead officer's horse bolted, running forward past Bella and Julio, and then continued on passing Sesasi.

The muskets reloaded, Julio retook his position and told Bella to reload the pistol she had fired. He could not have picked a more ideal spot to set up the ambush. If the soldiers kept coming forward one at a time, they would be easy to pick off, but none were brave enough to venture forth. With the officer in charge dead, the sergeant who was next in command ordered the rest of the unit to fall back.

Bella and Julio waited a long time, but no more soldiers appeared. After a respectful interval, Julio cautiously went to take a look, and saw that the trail was empty.

"Do we dare go back down?" Bella asked anxiously as she and Julio rejoined Sesasi and the horses.

"No. It is not safe. Those soldiers may be looking for another way to get around us. We do not know these mountains. We must go forward and try to find another way out of here before the soldiers find us."

The three companions mounted up and continued ascending the side of the mountain until the trail curved and began to descend. As daylight faded, they found a sheltered spot to spend the night. The temperature dropped as darkness fell, but they dared not risk making a fire. They sat huddled shoulder-to-shoulder, their backs to the stone wall, with all of their blankets covering them.

In the morning, with empty stomachs and no food in their saddle-bags, Bella, Julio and Sesasi mounted their horses and continued to descend into a narrow defile between the flanks of two peaks. "Where do we go from here?" Bella asked, riding beside Julio.

"Tejas."

"But is that not part of the Mexican Empire?"

"Yes, but it is a large territory, and few people. Hopefully we will find a place to live where no one will bother us."

Bella nodded. A place where no one would bother them. That sounded ideal to her. Glancing over her shoulder, however, she saw a dust cloud rising on the trail far behind them. "The soldiers," she said, pointing at the tell-tale sign of horses on the move.

"Yes," Julio agreed. They put bootheels to their horses' flanks and picked up the pace. As they traveled on throughout the morning, it became clear that their pursuers were gaining on them. Julio began looking for another spot to make a stand, but the defile they had traversed had opened into a broader valley. If they stopped to fight, the soldiers could come at them from all sides. There was no way of telling how many soldiers were in the troop. It was possible the unit had returned overnight to the fort outside of Santa Fe for reinforcements. Bella and the others goaded the horses into a gallop. It was now a race. All they could do was hope that the soldiers horses, having been spurred on to gain ground, would tire first.

The horses began to flag, but at least they had once again put distance between themselves and pursuing troopers. Am I really worth 500 silver pesos to them, Bella wondered, slowing Gabby to a walk. They came to a stream and dismounted to let the horses drink and rest. A grove of cottonwoods lined both banks of the stream. At that altitude their leaves were already turning yellow, although it was still late summer. It was beautiful country under a bright blue sky, but there was no time to appreciate nature's glory.

"If we push the horses, we will kill them," Julio said. "If we must fight, this is as good a place as any."

Bella looked at her two companions. She loved them both dearly. Sesasi had raised her from infancy, and Julio had taught her to ride, to duel, and to shoot. He had been to her what her father should have been. "I will give myself up," she said suddenly. "I am the one they are after. The two of you may be able to escape. Walk your horses up into the hills, into those trees. Perhaps the soldiers will be content to take me."

Julio shook his head, and Sesasi looked shocked at Bella's suggestion. "No, my Bellita," Julio said. "What will that accomplish? They will take you back to Santa Fe and hang you. How does that honor Alder? Do you think Sesasi and I traveled a thousand miles to find you and protect you, only to allow you to do this? When we left your father's hacienda to look for you, our only thought was to find you and help you escape the price on your head. Do you think we would abandon that goal now? No, we stand together and fight. If today we die, then we die together. Besides, it is better to go down fighting than to dangle at the end of a rope."

Sesasi nodded her agreement. There was nothing for it then but to prepare for battle. Julio urged Sesasi to take the horses into a thicket and remain hidden there with them, but she refused. She took the horses and

tethered them, but returned to do her bit in the coming fight. Julio and
Bella were hunkered down behind a fallen tree trunk, and Sesasi joined
them there. Then it was only a matter of waiting for the soldiers to arrive.

They waited and waited, but no soldiers put in their appearance. It
was late in the day, dark was settling in, and the soldiers, unaware that
their quarry was only a short distance ahead, had halted to rest their
horses and make camp for the night, intending to resume the pursuit
in the morning.

Finally, as full dark fell and a gibbous moon rose in the east, Bella and
the others saw the glow of the soldiers' fires no more than half a mile
away. Bella and Julio looked at each other in the light of the moon and
smiled. The three companions cautiously rose and found their tethered
horses. The horses, having been watered, and with several hours rest, were
fit to travel. Bella and the others walked their mounts across the stream
and down the far bank for some distance before climbing onto the saddles. Not wanting to create any noise that might carry in the still night
air, they set out at a leisurely trot, navigating the landscape by the sil-
very moonlight. It was not until they had traveled several miles that they
speeded up the horses.

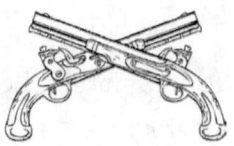

CHAPTER TWENTY-THREE

Bella, Julio, and Sesasi rode throughout the night headed south by east. By the time the eastern sky began to lighten, they were dead tired and ravenously hungry, but it appeared that their pursuers had been thrown off their track. There was no sign of the soldiers trailing behind. They came upon an isolated farm, nothing more than a shack and a few dilapidated outbuildings. A curl of smoke wafted from the crude stone chimney. They approached warily, not wanting to alarm the residents. Bella dismounted and approached the door. "*Hola!*" she called out. There was no response. She rapped on the door, but no one answered. When she pulled on the door, it swung open on sagging leather hinges. There was no one inside, but a pot of beans was simmering in a cast iron kettle over a small fire, and corn tortillas were stacked on a rickety table. The only other furnishings were two chairs by the table and two narrow mats lying a few feet apart in the back corner.

A few chickens and a scrawny rooster scratched in the dirt behind the house. Sesasi climbed down from her horse and found three eggs hidden in clumps of dried grass. "No one is inside," Bella reported, "but there are beans cooking, so someone is around."

Julio dismounted then and tethered the three horses to a fence rail. Just then a young girl appeared from around the corner of the house. She looked to be around twelve or thirteen, and was wearing a faded dress. Her dark hair dangled over her shoulders in two long braids. She was carrying a wooden bucket of water and froze at the sight of the three strangers.

"Hello, I am Bella. We mean you no harm," Bella said in Spanish. The girl looked as though she did not understand.

"I think she is Indian," Julio said. "Navajo, perhaps."

"Yes," Sesasi agreed.

Bella tried to communicate with signs that they were hungry, and taking several silver Pesos out of her money pouch, offered them to the girl in exchange for food. The girl just stared wide-eyed.

A minute later an old man emerged from a stand of trees east of the house. He, too, looked more Indian than Spanish. He wore much-patched trousers, a woolen poncho, and a dirty wide-brimmed hat. He, too, froze at the sight of Bella, Julio and Sesasi.

Bella called out a greeting in Spanish. "We mean you no harm. We are travelers and are hungry." She held out her open hand displaying the silver coins. "We will pay for food."

The old man's eyes widened at the sight of the money. He clearly understood Bella's Spanish, but spoke to the girl in a strange language. The girl continued to stare for a moment, and then went inside the shack. The man approached cautiously, taking note of the strangers' weapons.

"We are not here to rob you. We have ridden all night. We are tired and hungry," Bella said, giving the old man a warm smile. "Will you sell us food? May we rest here a little while?"

The girl emerged from the hut bearing two tin plates and a pottery bowl, all filled with beans and tortillas. Shyly, she passed plates to Bella and Julio, and the bowl to Sesasi. There were hand-carved wooden spoons for each guest.

"I am Sicheii," the old man said in Spanish, and nodding to the girl, "She is Ajei, my granddaughter. She understands a little Spanish, but is very shy. We are Navajo. I have sheep up there." He pointed to a hillside beyond the clump of trees.

Despite being half-starved, Bella handed him the silver Pesos before starting in on the beans. The girl, noting that Sesasi had found three eggs, took them from her and returned to the house. A few minutes later she returned holding an iron skillet, and slid a fried egg onto the tops of each guest's pile of beans.

Bella, Julio, and Sesasi ate standing up; Julio leaned against the decrepit fence where the horses were tethered. They had been in the saddle all night and it felt good to stand. It felt even better to get food into their empty, growling stomachs.

Sicheii silently watched the three companions eat, and Ajei stood by his side, her grandfather's arm draped across her shoulders. When the guests were finished eating, Ajei collected their plates and spoons.

"Why have you ridden all night?" Sicheii finally asked.

Bella hesitated a moment before answering. She thought about making something up, but then decided that the truth, at least mostly the truth, would serve them best. "Soldiers are chasing us. They believe we are outlaws, but we are not."

The old man spat in the dirt. "Soldiers," he said with contempt. "Where are the soldiers when the Comanche raid? Where were they when Ajei's mother and father were murdered by the Comanche? Where are the soldiers when the Comanche steal my sheep? Even if you are outlaws, I would help you escape the soldiers."

"We need to sleep," Julio said.

"Take your horses and go into those trees. You will be hidden there. If soldiers come, I will tell them you passed through here yesterday."

"Is it only you and your granddaughter here?" Bella asked.

"Sadly, yes. She is my heart. That is the meaning of her name."

Bella followed Julio and Sesasi who were leading the horses into the copse of cottonwoods. After tethering the horses, Bella stretched out on the ground and fell asleep almost immediately. Julio and Sesasi lay together on a blanket and also slept, trusting Sicheii would not betray them.

Early in the afternoon, Bella awoke to the clop, clop, clop of horses' hooves. She crawled on hands and knees to the edge of the thicket and saw half a dozen mounted soldiers in the dirt yard in front of the shack. An officer was talking to Sicheii, showing him a piece of paper. She realized it was her wanted poster. So much for helping them escape. The old man may have had no love for Spanish soldiers, but apparently the reward of 500 silver pesos was too tempting; Sicheii pointed to the stand of trees at the edge of his land.

"Julio, quick!" Bella shouted, drawing her pistols. There was no point in trying to be stealthy, the soldiers were already guiding their horses toward the patch of woods. In a minute Julio was by her side, carrying the two muskets. He fired one, and Bella shot her two pistols. Two of the six soldiers fell. Julio fired the second musket, bringing down another soldier as he tried to dismount.

Bella's spare powder and balls were stowed in her satchel hung from Gabby's saddle. Julio handed her one of his two pistols. He, Bella and Sesasi lay flat on the ground as the remaining three soldiers foolishly fired their carbines into the woods, without having well-defined targets. Realizing the soldiers would have to reload, Bella leapt to her feet and broke out of the woods, followed closely by Julio and Sesasi. Wielding pistols, all three fired, felling another soldier. The officer drew a pistol and shot at Julio, striking him in the shoulder. Bella pulled her rapier and ran at the officer, who drew his own sword.

They squared off, Bella and the captain, facing each other with their swords, each making feints, looking for an opening. The remaining soldier was ramming a lead ball down the barrel of his carbine when Sesasi came at him with a long knife. The soldier swung the butt of his gun at her, but she ducked and rising up, let out a whoop, and drove the knife into the man's belly. He staggered back and fell to his knees, then forward onto his face.

Bella and the officer danced around each other, crossing blades. The captain, an experienced swordsman, deftly wielded his saber, and Bella was unable to penetrate his defenses. In like manner, however, Bella parried the captain's every thrust. Julio, his shoulder shattered, could only watch as his protégé dueled the Spanish officer. Finally, the captain thrust toward Bella's midsection, and when she deflected his blade up and to the right, its tip sliced upward across her cheek, opening a gash from her dimpled chin to just under her eye. Blood poured from the wound down the side of her face and neck. Thinking he had defeated the impertinent girl, the wanted outlaw who had dared cross blades with him, he momentarily lowered his guard, and Bella drove the tip of her sword straight through his chest, piercing his heart. He fell with a shocked expression frozen on his face.

Sesasi had started attending to Julio's shoulder, but she let out a shriek when she saw Bella's bloody face. "My Bella," she cried.

"I will be okay," Bella said, drawing her sword from the dead captain's body, but when she placed her hand to the side of her face, and it came away covered in blood, she realized the cut was more than a mere scratch.

Suddenly there was another shriek as Ajei came out of the cabin and saw her grandfather lying in a pool of blood on the ground. Bella thought a stray pistol ball had missed its mark and struck the old man, but Sesasi spoke up and said, "I shot him for betraying us."

There was nothing more to be said. Bella, holding a strip cut from her petticoat to the side of her face, sat down on what passed for a stoop leading to the cabin door. "See to Julio," she told Sesasi, but Julio insisted Bella be treated first.

Sesasi retrieved needle and thread from her bags. "My poor Bella, I must sew your wound," she said. "Your beautiful face will be scarred."

"I know. Do it," Bella replied. Julio had a flagon of clear liquor in his saddlebags, so Sesasi soaked a piece of cloth and daubed at Bella's cheek. The alcohol burned like fire. Bella tried to hold as still as possible, but could not help wincing with each stitch Sesasi put in. Tears squirted from her closed eyes; the pain was intense.

Sesasi wrapped a bandage around Bella's head, over the top and under her jaw to cover the wound, and then returned to tend to Julio's shoulder. The pistol ball was embedded in his shoulder, shattering the bone and tearing tendons. Sesasi dug the lead ball out with the tip of her knife, and then cleaned the wound and sewed it closed. She bandage Julio's shoulder and fashioned a sling. All the while, Ajei knelt at her grandfather's side, weeping.

Bella stood and went to the girl, laying her hand on Ajei's shoulder. "I am sorry your grandfather is dead. Your grandfather said you have no one else. You must come with us." The girl looked up with a tear-stained face, but said nothing.

"The soldiers must have split up into small units to widen the search," Julio said. We have to get moving."

Several of the soldiers' horses had fled, but two remained standing nearby. Sesasi brought the horses to the fence and tethered them while she fetched her horse, Julio's and Bella's from the copse of cottonwoods. Bella retrieved the silver Pesos she had paid Sicheii for his hospitality. He no longer had need of them. They took whatever was useful from inside the cabin and secured it to the back of one of the military horses. Bella helped Ajei onto the saddle of the other horse; the small, slender girl sat astride the tall horse, looking numb. Sesasi was against taking the girl with them, but Bella would not consider leaving the child behind all alone. Julio and Bella dragged Sicheii's body inside the shack, and then set the shack on fire. Smoke billowed into the still air as they rode away, leading the pack horse and the one Ajei sat. The girl looked back once over her shoulder at the flaming structure that had been her home, and then, facing forward, followed the three strangers who had brought death and destruction into her young life.

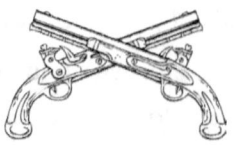

CHAPTER TWENTY-FOUR

J ulio was worried that smoke from the burning cabin would draw the other patrols of soldiers, so he and the others rode hard and fast going south and east the rest of the day, headed for Texas. Ajei lagged behind, and several times the others had to stop to allow her to catch up. Fortunately, there was no sign that they were being pursued. Bella and her companions were in no shape for another fight. With his left shoulder shattered, and his arm in a sling, Julio could not hold a musket. Bella's wound made her half sick with pain, as though her face was on fire. They camped for the night under the stars, and dined on re-heated beans and roasted chicken, having caught several of the chickens at Sicheii's homestead. Sesasi wrung the scrawny rooster's neck and roast-ed the tough old bird skewered on a stick over the fire.

Ajei sat apart from the others, quietly watching. Bella tried to get the girl to join the rest of the party, but she refused. Bella began to think they might have been better off leaving the girl behind. She seemed capable of taking care of herself, and Bella began to regret burning the shack. Bella hoped the girl would eventually come around. Little did Bella or the others know that Ajei understood much more Spanish than she or her grandfather had let on. She had clearly heard Sesasi proclaim that she deliberately killed Sicheii because he had betrayed them.

That night, while Sesasi was on watch, letting Bella and Julio rest, Ajei silently crept up behind her. She clamped her hand over Sesasi's mouth and plunged a knife into her lower back, piercing Sesasi's kidney and liver. In shock, Sesasi slumped forward and did not even cry out. Ajei then slit Sesasi's throat. Having taken revenge for the death of her grandfather, Ajei walked one of the soldiers' horses out of camp. Once she was away from camp, she swung onto the horse's back, and clutching its mane, galloped off.

Bella awoke first in the morning. She stood, stretched, rubbed the sleep from her eyes, and then froze as she saw Sesasi lying on the ground, unmoving, a dark pool of drying blood surrounding her body.

"Oh no!" Bella cried. "Oh God, please no!" She went to Sesasi's side and fell to her knees. Hot tears flooded her eyes as she stared at the lifeless form of the woman who had practically raised her.

Julio stirred. "What is it?" he asked, struggling to sit up. Blood had seeped through his shoulder bandage.

"No, no, no!" Bella wailed. "She's dead, Julio! Sesasi is dead!"

"What?" Julio could scarcely believe what he was hearing. How could that be? How could the woman he had quietly come to love be dead.

"It was Ajei," Bella said, her shoulders sagging. "She must have heard Sesasi say she killed her grandfather."

"I will hunt that girl!" Julio said angrily, getting to his feet. "I will kill her!"

"No, Julio. Ajei is gone. She took one of the horses. Killing her will not bring Sesasi back." Tears were streaming down Bella's left cheek and wetting the bandage on right one. "Am I to lose everyone I love?"

Julio walked to Bella's side and knelt next to her by Sesasi's lifeless body. "I am still with you, Bellita." He put his good arm around her shoulders, and Bella rested her head against the side of his chest.

They dug a shallow grave and laid Sesasi's body to rest. They mounded dirt and then rocks over the grave. Bella made a crude cross of two pieces of pine branch, and Julio pounded it into the ground at the head of the grave using the butt of a pistol as a hammer.

"She was Catholic," Bella said, and then prayed the Our Father and a Hail Mary over the grave. In no mood to eat, Bella and Julio packed what they could on their horses. After releasing Sesasi's horse and the other military horse to roam free, they rode off, headed for Texas.

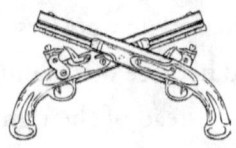

CHAPTER TWENTY-FIVE

For the next three years Bella and Julio roamed the West. The wound to Bella's face healed, but the ugly, raised scar it left forever marred her beauty. They traveled back and forth across Texas, returned to New Mexico—the southern part of the territory, avoiding Santa Fe— and entered the Arizona portion of the Mexican Empire, and finally back to Texas again. They tried unsuccessfully to locate Kuruk's tribe, but the nomadic band of Apaches had moved often in the pursuit of game.

Bella's brief pregnancy ended in miscarriage. After fleeing Santa Fe she was consumed with grief after having seen Alder cut down by soldiers' musket fire, and on top of that there was the tragic loss of her beloved Sesasi. It had been almost too much to bear. Julio was her only remaining friend in the entire world. She vowed she would never again become romantically involved with any man unless they were in a stable, loving relationship, and not on the run from the authorities.

For the most part the pair managed to avoid contact with the Comanche and the Mexican military. Quick shooting and fast horses got them out of several close calls. They had more than one narrow escape. Bella remained a wanted desperado, and new posters distributed throughout the Mexico territories depicted her face with a much exaggerated scar, oddly on the left side of her face instead of the right. She eventually got used to people staring at her scar, and found that the evidence of her wound instilled both fear and respect in the citizens she encountered. Her reputation as a dangerous outlaw exceeded the reality, but in most instances, her notoriety worked to her benefit.

Julio's shoulder never properly healed. His left arm became almost useless, and he was in nearly constant pain. Life on the run was hard on him, constantly looking over his shoulder, trying to hang onto reins while shooting with only one good hand. Bella was twenty, young and strong, whereas Julio was by then in his sixties. He took up drinking to dull the pain in his shattered shoulder.

Bella sometimes teased him, calling him "Old Man," but she worried about him constantly. She chided him about his drinking, but understood it helped him cope with the pain of his wound and the aches and pains of his aging body. It was getting harder and harder for him to keep up with her, and he resented the fact that he was no longer young and agile. He had developed a dry cough that would not go away. Julio stopped calling her Bellita the day she received her wound. Being cut by the Spanish captain's sword had changed her, hardened her. For a time she lost confidence in her dueling capability, but she began practicing relentlessly to hone her skills, vowing that never again would she allow an opponent to touch her with his blade.

Bella's money eventually ran out, and she and Julio tried to find work, but with a price on her head, taking a job in a town was too risky, and there was little work to be found on the scattered ranchos of West Texas. To survive, she and Julio were eventually forced to turn to robbery.

They robbed supply wagons, or travelers' coaches, taking only what they needed to get by. They did not try to get rich, and did their best to avoid injuring anyone, but sometimes that could not be avoided. Occasionally men resisted, and if gunplay ensued, it was always the luckless victim left lying in the dust. Bella's reputation as a deadly pistol shot and swordswoman grew, and on the rare occasions when she walked into a cantina, other patrons gave her wide berth.

Although Bella generally wore a mask over her lower face when engaged in robbery, her identity was widely known, and her scar was partially visible above the mask. There was only one highwaywoman operating on the western high plains, and the bounty on her head was upped from 500 silver Pesos to 100 gold Doubloons. There was an equal price placed on Julio, also wanted dead or alive.

Bella's girlish dreams of leading a quiet, peaceful life had long since fallen by the wayside. The only life she knew was spending long days in the saddle, and trying to avoid capture or confrontation. A few intrepid men, lured by the promise of a rich reward, tried their luck at bringing her down, but none survived the encounters. Being always wary, always on guard was exhausting, and as the time passed, Julio was becoming more of a burden than a help.

"You should leave me," he would often say, especially after a violent coughing spell, or when his body was so wracked with aches and pains it was difficult for him to mount a horse, let alone spend an entire day in the saddle.

Bella always replied, "Never."

Never does not always mean never. On a hot, humid afternoon, not far from the Texas Gulf Coast, Bella and Julio rode into a dusty little village. Julio had been coughing up a little blood, which he tried to conceal from Bella, but she knew he was not at all well. Taking a big risk, they rented a room above a cantina. While Bella took a much needed bath, Julio stretched out atop the bed to rest. He suffered a violent fit of coughing, and when Bella returned from bathing, she found him feverish, sweating profusely, and with flecks of blood spattered on the front of his shirt.

"Oh, Julio," she said, sitting on the edge of the mattress next to him. She brushed a straggly lock of steel gray hair away from his damp forehead. She helped him sit up and unbuttoned his shirt, easing it off of him. She helped him put on a less dirty shirt from his saddlebag. "I will get soup," she said.

He grabbed her wrist. "Bring whiskey."

"And soup." Bella went downstairs to the main room, carrying her pistols, of course. Her guns were never out of reach. She was aware that every eye in the place was on her as she crossed to the bar. "A bottle of whiskey, and soup and bread to take up to the room." She slapped several silver Pesos on the counter.

The barkeep passed her a bottle of rot-gut booze, and told her he would send a serving girl to the room with the food. Out of the corner of her eye, Bella noticed a man slip furtively out the front door. Three years of being constantly on guard had made her wary of everyone, but Julio was seriously ill, too ill to leave the cantina, too ill to get out of bed. She took the whiskey up to the room and, after pouring a generous drink into a glass, handed it to her oldest and dearest friend, her only friend. He took a long draught of the fiery liquor and a faint smile spread across his face.

There was a knock at the door. Bella drew a pistol and unlocked and cautiously opened the door. A wide-eyed girl of twelve or so was standing outside with a tray—two bowls of soup, and bread. Bella took the tray and handed the girl a silver Peso. She again sat by Julio's side on the edge of the bed and hand-fed him spoonful after spoonful of soup, until he finally pushed her hand away.

"Pour more whiskey," he said.

"You need to eat."

Julio looked Bella in the eye. "My Bellita, I am dying." It was the first time he had called her that in three years. "Soup will not cure me. Neither will whiskey, but at least it makes me feel better."

"No, no, you are sick, but you will get better."

"I will not. This is the end for me, my dear girl. I will not leave this bed. I am certain of it. I love you, my Bella. I loved you as a little girl, and I have loved you every day since, but you have to let me go now."

"No, I cannot. I will not."

"You have no choice. My body is at its end. I have no regrets. I have killed men, and robbed, but I have been with you to protect you and help you. That is enough for me. Now you will be on your own, and I am sorry I will no longer be at your side, but you are strong, Bella, and resourceful." Just then there was the sound of boots tramping up the stairs.

Bella started to draw her pistols, but Julio grabbed her wrists. "Give me my pistols," he demanded. "Go, now, climb out the window. Quickly."

"No, I will not leave you."

"Yes, you must. Please, I beg you. Do this last thing for me. Escape. Live. Let me serve you one last time."

Bella hesitated a moment, but the heavy footsteps were at the top of the landing. A hand tried turning the doorknob, but Bella had relocked the stout door.

"Go! Go now!" Julio said, pushing Bella away. She handed him his pistols and took one last look at her dear friend, before turning to the window. It was full dark out. She opened the window and stepped onto the tile eave overhanging the front of the cantina. The door to the room crashed open, and there were two quick pistol shots, followed by a half dozen more. Bella knew the second volley had ended Julio's life.

She ran along the rooftop and leaped down. Her horse and Julio's were stabled behind the cantina, but there was no time to saddle Gabby to escape. A large Palomino gelding was tethered to a hitching rail at the end of the cantina. Without hesitation Bella leaped onto the horse's back, putting her heels to its flanks. Several shots rang out behind her, but she kept low over the horse's neck. The Palomino was a very fast horse.

Bella rode at a break-neck gallop until she was certain she was far enough away from the village that no one would come after her that night. They, whoever they were, the nameless, faceless men who were forever chasing her would pursue her as soon as it was light, and so she needed to keep going. She slowed the horse to a walk and continued on, and as her heart rate slowed, and the rush of adrenaline faded, she sat in the saddle completely numb. Julio was dead. Even though she had not seen it, she could picture him lying on the bed, riddled with bullets. She knew he had fired first to give her a chance to escape, and hoped he had taken one or two of the men with him to the grave. She was alone. Everyone she had ever loved was dead. She was on her own, still hunted, always hunted. Most of her belongings were left behind in the room. All she had were the clothes she wore, her pistols and rapier, and a handful of pesos in the pocket of her skirt.

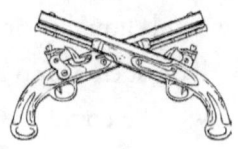

CHAPTER TWENTY-SIX

Just before first light Bella stopped to rest. She dismounted and checked the horse's saddlebags. There was a little jerked beef, a man's shirt, a small cloth bag with a few pesos jingling inside, a powder flask, and a leather pouch with a handful of lead pistol balls. She walked the Palomino to the top of a bluff, and for the first time in her life, viewed the sea. Even though she had grown up in Old Mexico, essentially a huge peninsula between the Caribbean Sea and the Sea of Cortez, she had never seen the ocean. It had never occurred to her father to take his daughter on a frivolous trip to the seashore.

Sea birds were soaring above the water, and the sun was rising out of the sea in the east, casting shimmering bands of red and gold on the waves. Bella was enchanted. She quietly stared at the scene. Below her, in a sheltered cove, a twin-masted ship was anchored, its sails furled. A rowboat was drawn up on the beach, and men were loading it with crates and barrels. A second rowboat, similarly laden, was halfway between land and the vessel, being rowed from shore to the waiting ship.

Entranced, Bella stood at the top of the cliff, watching the activity on the beach below, and a wistful thought entered her mind. How wonderful it would be to embark on such a ship and simply sail away from all of her troubles and sorrows. She could see exotic lands she had only read about in the books in her father's library, England, France, Italy, and especially Spain, her mother's birthplace. She could travel to places where she was unknown, where there was no price on her head, where she could start an entirely new life. She sighed. I doubt they would take a woman on board, she thought, and if they would, what might happen to me? She would probably be the only woman on a ship full of lusty men. She could defend herself, of course, and had done so many times, but against an entire ship's crew with no means of escape?

Suddenly Bella was startled out of her reverie by the thunder of approaching horses' hooves. Three groups of riders were descending on her from three directions, directly behind, and on both flanks. There were at least a dozen men in total, and there was nowhere for her to go. In front of her was a steep, rocky bluff rising above the beach.

Bella leapt onto the Palomino's back and pulled out her pistols. I will die here today, she thought, but they will pay in blood to collect the reward. She was about to ride out to meet her pursuers head on, but suddenly spotted a narrow, tortuous trail descending from the top of the cliff to the beach. Standing, she had not been able to see the trail, but from the higher perspective of horseback, it was plainly visible. Sticking her pistols back into her sash, she jerked the reins, turning the horse's head to the right. She put heels to the horse's flanks, and the big gelding leapt forward over the edge of the clifftop.

The horse was sure-footed, and Bella was an expert rider. Nevertheless, it was a hair-raising ride down the switchback trail. One misstep would send horse and rider plummeting over the side to their deaths on the rocks below.

The posse that was chasing Bella consisted of half a dozen soldiers and an equal number of civilians eager for a share of the reward on her head. Startled by Bella's sudden disappearance over the edge of the bluff, they reined in their horses expecting to see their quarry dashed to pieces on the rocky beach. Several soldiers dismounted, and when they peered down the cliff face, they saw Bella flying along the trail with reckless speed.

Three of the soldiers fired their muskets at her, but missed by a mile. Their officer, a lieutenant, eased his horse through the brush that hid the trail's entrance, and followed Bella's route, but at a less daring pace. Two more soldiers and three of the civilians followed suit, riding single file.

As soon as Bella hit the beach, she quickly dismounted and drew her pistols. It was there she would make her stand, her last stand she assumed. There was nowhere else to go except into the ocean; the beach was not broad and was flanked at both ends by rocky outcroppings of the cliff behind. Although Bella had learned how to swim, the Caribbean Sea was vast. There was nowhere to swim to, no opposite shore in sight. The men chasing her were forced to ride single file on the narrow trail. Needing to be mindful of guiding their horses' steps, they would be unable to shoot accurately until they, too, reached the beach. Bella had only her two pistols, the gifts from Julio when she was a girl. She figured she could probably pick off the lead two, but that still left four men, and it was unlikely they would be courteous enough to engage her in sword fights, one at a time, or allow her the opportunity to reload her guns.

She glanced sideways down the beach where the rowboat was being loaded. The boat was at least a hundred yards away. Could she make a dash for the boat? What would that buy her? It was possible that the men loading the boat would turn her in for the reward. If I die, she thought, I will see Alder, Julio, and Sesasi again, wherever they may be. It was unlikely the meeting would take place in Heaven. Still, a little Catholic superstition could not hurt. Briefly casting her eyes skyward, she mumbled aloud, "Forgive me," and made the sign of the cross over her breast.

The lieutenant in the lead reached the beach and charged, brandishing a pistol. Bella shot him out of the saddle. The next soldier, leaning low over his horse's neck to make a smaller target, rode hard straight at Bella. Her second pistol shot shattered his knee, and as he started to fall, the horse went down with him, landing atop its rider.

Bella defiantly drew her rapier and waited for the other four riders to come at her. All four men wielded pistols, and Bella expected to be cut down in a hail of gunfire at any moment. Shots rang out, but they came from behind her, not from her pursuers. Startled, she watched as two of her pursuers fell from their horses. Bella turned her head and saw a tall, redhaired man sporting a thick, full beard, just as fiery as the hair on his head, standing not fifty feet away. With him was another man, shorter, stockier, with a tangle of wiry, steel gray hair, and wearing a plaid cap, similar to a beret. He was leveling a brace of pistols at the remaining two of Bella's pursuers, but withheld his fire when the last two riders turned and beat a hasty retreat back up the bluff the way they had come.

The two men from the boat approached Bella. Still holding her rapier at the ready, she watched them warily. Just because they had saved her from her pursuers, did not mean they were not interested in collecting for themselves the reward for her death or capture.

"*Hola, Señorita*," the tall redhaired man said. That was about the extent of his Spanish. He pointed at himself and said, "Ned O'Keeffe,"

"I am Isabella Vasquez. I speak some English."

Ned looked relieved. "This here is Mac." He nodded at the man next to him.

"Angus MacGregor," the man said, tucking his pistols into a broad leather belt. "I think you'd better come with us, Lassie."

"Where?"

"Anywhere but here," Ned replied. He had taken a spyglass out of a leather case attached to his belt, and after extending it, scanned the clifftop. "I count seven or eight of those men still up there waiting to see what happens. Why are they after you? You steal that big old tan horse?"

"Yes." Bella hesitated. "There is a price on my head."

Ned let out a hearty laugh. "Mine, too. Me and my crew, we're pirates. That brigantine anchored there is my ship, the *Queen Maeve*. I'm the Captain, Red Ned. You look like you know what you're doing with that sword, and you can definitely shoot. You're welcome to come aboard and join us if you like, or we can put you off wherever you want, but you can't go back up that trail unless you're hell bent on dying."

"You can put that sword away, Lassie," Mac told her. "We aren't going to hurt you."

Again Bella hesitated. Pirates. The two men looked friendly enough, but joining a pirate crew? She knew Ned was right. There was no escape from the beach other than by the rowboat. If she tried to fight her way free from the men waiting at the top of the cliff, she would be killed or captured, and capture meant being hung. There were just too many of them. If she remained on the beach alone, the men would eventually come down to her. Better to take my chances on the *Queen Maeve*, she thought. She slowly sheathed her rapier.

"I will go with you, Captain Red Ned. You may call me Bella."

"Okay, Bella, it looks as though my men have the rest of the supplies loaded onto the boat, so let's get going before the tide turns."

Bella followed the two men across the wet sand, taking the precaution of reloading and priming her pistols while she walked, a skill she had developed during her years on the run. If I join this crew, I will still be wanted, she thought, but I will be harder to find and harder to catch. Maybe I will get to see some of the world. Still, her stomach was fluttering anxiously as she climbed into the boat with six strange men. Four were manning the oars, and they gave her hard looks, lustful looks, it seemed to her, and she could not help wondering what she had gotten herself into. Ned and Mac shoved the boat off the sand. Mac went to the bow, and Ned extended his hand to Bella, helping her settle onto a seat at the stern. She had never before been in a boat of any kind. Ned sat by her side and took control of the tiller. Bella watched the men row, their strokes smooth and coordinated. In short order they reached the side of the ship. Mac secured the boat to a mooring ring, and climbed up a rope ladder to the main deck. The rowers shipped their oars, and began securing the crates and barrels to ropes thrown down from the ship's rail.

"Up you go, Miss Vasquez," Ned said.

Bella took a deep breath and began climbing the swaying rope ladder. Ned followed close behind her. As Bella stepped over the rail onto the deck, she was met with the stares of dozens of men.

Ned threw his long legs over the side, looked around at his crew, and announced, "Men, this here is Bella Vasquez. She's our guest, and is under my protection. Any man who bothers her answers to me." Taking Bella by the arm, he told her, "Come to the cabin with me. We'll get you something to eat."

As Bella walked with Ned toward the rear of the ship, she looked around at the strange new world she had just entered, and again wondered what she had gotten herself into.

Part Four

A PIRATE

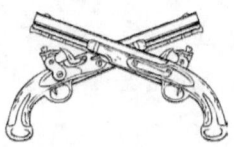

CHAPTER TWENTY-SEVEN

"So, Miss Bella, why are you wanted?" Ned asked, eating stew from a silver bowl with a silver spoon. Bella tasted the stew a crewmen had set before her. It was pretty good, she thought, much better than she would have expected on a pirate ship, better than she could have made herself, not that she was much of a cook. There was fresh baked bread as well, and mugs of ale to wash it down.

In between spoonfuls of beefy stew, and chunks of bread still warm from the oven, Bella related an abbreviated version of her story from the time she left her father's hacienda to her appearance on the beach that morning. She did not mention Alder, but spoke of Julio Higuera and Sesasi, her companions in flight, saying only that they had died without mentioning the details of their passing.

"So, how many men have you killed?" Ned asked, a little incredulous.

"I have no idea. I did not keep count."

Ned was skeptical of her claims, but his disbelief began to change when, after a knock on the door, a dark-haired man entered the cabin. He had a bushy moustache, a patch over his left eye, and a scarred upper lip curled into a permanent sneer.

The man drew up short when he spotted Bella. He had been below deck supervising the storing of supplies when Bella came aboard. "Captain what's a woman doing on board?" he demanded, staring at Bella, assuming she was some plaything the captain had picked up ashore.

"Bella, this is my First Mate, John Carver. John, this is Miss Isabella Vasquez. She may join our crew, or at least sail with us for a while."

Carver glared intently at Bella, and she calmly and steadfastly returned his gaze. In the end Carver blinked first and looked away. He spat out, "Bah. A woman on a ship is bad luck. Mark my word, she'll be a Jonah."

Bella was quite familiar with the Old Testament story of Jonah, and resented the implication that she was a bad luck talisman. The fact that Bella had outstared the meanest pirate in the crew told Ned more about her than words could have ever expressed. "John, Miss Vasquez is my guest. See to getting the ship ready to sail at the turn of the tide."

Carver nodded his head, keeping his eyes averted from Bella's continuing stare. "The supplies are stowed. The ship will be ready to sail." With that, he turned on his heel and left the room.

"Be careful, you've just made an enemy, and a dangerous one, too," Ned commented, noticing that Bella's hand had disappeared under the table when Carver entered, to grasp one of her pistols he assumed. He had seen her proficiency with pistols on the beach.

Bella shrugged. "Many men have been my enemy." She gave Ned a half smile. "A few are still alive."

Ned laughed. "You know, I think I believe you."

Bella decided she might be able to like this huge, shaggy, redhaired man. She began to think that perhaps it just might be possible that she could begin to trust him. She wanted to know more about him and the ship before deciding to join his crew. "Tell me, Captain Ned O'Keeffe, how is it you are Captain of this ship, and how you came to be a pirate."

"Ah, there's a tale," Ned replied, pouring himself and Bella more ale from a pewter pitcher. "I'm an Irishman, born and raised in Galway, on the west coast of Ireland. I left home to go to sea as a cabin boy on a merchantman when I was twelve. That was quite a while ago. When the British colonies in North America rebelled, in '76, I signed onto this ship as a crewman. No love lost between me and the British. Those bloody bastards occupy my country and call it their own. They need to get the hell out of Ireland.

"Back in those days, this ship was owned and captained by a Frenchman, the Comte DeGuillard. It was called the *Liberte'* at that time. As you may know, France helped the Americans in their war. We ran guns and supplies to the colonies. We were what they called a privateer. I guess I did a good job, because DeGuillard made me his First Mate.

"One day we had a run in with a British warship, and were boarded by Royal Marines. Before we repelled them and got away, one of them marines tried to run DeGuillard through with a sword, but I stepped in and killed the blasted Limey, saving my captain's life.

"When the war was over, in '83, and the Americans had licked those Redcoat bastards, DeGuillard decided to retire to his estate in France. He was getting on in years and his health was poor. In gratitude for saving his life, and because he liked me, sort of thought of me as the son he never had, he gave me ownership of this ship. He booked passage on a French merchant ship and sailed away. I heard later that he died a year after returning home.

"Most of the crew was French, and didn't want to sail under an Irishman. They left, and I had to recruit a new crew. At first I thought I'd try my hand at carrying cargo, but this ship isn't big enough to compete with the merchant fleet, and it really isn't designed for hauling goods. She's sleek, built for speed, and she carries twelve heavy cannons, six on each side. When I couldn't make a go of it running a commercial vessel, I turned to piracy. I changed the ship's name to the *Queen Maeve*. And there you have it, that's my story."

"Who is Queen Maeve?" Bella asked, setting aside her empty bowl. It felt good to have a full belly. It had been a while since her last hot meal.

"Queen Maeve is, or rather was, an ancient Irish warrior queen. I don't know if she ever really existed, but I like to think she did. I figured it was a good name for my ship. Maybe someday I'll be able to use her to help drive the Bloody Brits out of my country."

Ned had been surreptitiously studying Bella while they ate, avoiding staring at the scar running almost the entire length of the right side of her face. No doubt that without the scar she would be a ravishingly beautiful young woman, perhaps the most beautiful woman he had ever seen, next to his Molly, of course. Molly had been the dark-haired love of Ned's life, but she had died in childbirth four years earlier, giving birth to the daughter Ned had abandoned after entrusting the infant into the care of his spinster older sister, Mary. Even with her scarred face, however, Bella was a comely woman. The question was, what to do with her? Where to put her? She could not very well sleep on the crew deck with nearly fifty men.

Bella was thinking along the same lines, and questioned her choice to come aboard the ship, the only woman among a crew of lusty pirates. She also wondered about Ned's intentions toward her. Although he tried to disguise it, she was well aware that he had been studying her features.

To break the tense feeling that had arisen after their meal was finished, Bella deliberately ran her finger down the length of her scar. "Sometimes it still bothers me," she said, casually, giving Ned an opening to probe deeper into her past.

"How did you get that?" he asked.

"In a duel with an officer of the Spanish army. He cut my face, but I ran him through. I was only seventeen. I was good with a sword then, but I am much better now."

"I don't know where to put you on the ship. Don't get the wrong idea, but if you don't mind, for the time being you can share the cabin with me. I will hang a hammock for you on the far side of the room."

"Are you being a gentleman, or do you find my scar repulsive?"

Ned laughed. "No one ever accused me of being a gentleman, and no, your scar doesn't bother me." He hesitated a minute. "I was married. Molly was the love of my life. She died four years ago. I guess I'm still not over her."

"I am sorry, Captain O'Keeffe. I, too, lost someone I loved. He died saving my life. If you do not mind, yes, I will share the cabin with you."

"The rest of the crew might get the wrong idea."

It was Bella's turn to laugh. "My Captain, I am wanted for the killing of a great number of men and for robbery. I do not worry about my reputation among your crew."

"It's settled then, for now I will have a hammock hung in here for you. I hope you don't mind, but I've been told I snore."

"And I've been told I sleep like a baby."

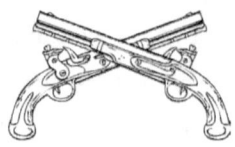

CHAPTER TWENTY-EIGHT

Bella awoke in the morning to a strange sensation. She was lying fully dressed in a hammock that was swaying gently back and forth. She stood and was unsteady on her feet. Ned was already up and out of the cabin. He had snored throughout the night, waking her several times, but each time she managed to fall back asleep. Her stomach felt queasy, and the plate of bread and jam left for her on the table did not look as appetizing as it otherwise might have.

Taking a pass on breakfast, she left the cabin. The ship was rolling side-to-side, and pitching fore and aft. The full array of sails were billowing in a strong breeze. The shore was barely visible on the horizon off the left side of the ship. Suddenly feeling nauseous, Bella staggered to the rail and threw up over the side. When she turned around, a number of crewmen taking a break from their duties to watch this strange woman heave over the rail, were having a good laugh at her expense. Only one man looked familiar, the second man from the beach who had come to her aid, Mac.

"There, there, Lassie. You'll get your sea legs soon enough," he said with a grin, giving her a gentle pat on the shoulder. Come below, I'll make you a cup of tea to settle your stomach."

Bella hesitated a moment, but the man seemed friendly enough. He was armed only with a knife, and she was carrying her two pistols and sword. She followed him through a hatch and down a ladder to the first deck below, the gun deck. Bella took note of the twelve large cannons secured with heavy ropes, six on each side of the ship. The gun ports were closed and locked, and barrels of gunpowder and crates of cannonballs were neatly arranged next to each gun.

"This here is the gun deck, and I'm the chief gunner and armorer aboard," Mac said over his shoulder as he lead Bella forward between the rows of cannons towards the bow. They reached a closed door in the forward bulkhead which Mac unlocked with a big iron key. "This is the arsenal where we store extra weapons. You help yourself to whatever powder and shot you need."

Bella peered inside. The room was roughly triangular. The walls curved inward, following the lines of the hull, and came to a point at the bow. A rack along one side held a row of muskets. The opposite wall held scores of pistols hanging on pegs. A big oak barrel was filled with swords of various types. There was a hammock suspended from the ceiling.

"This is where I bunk," Mac said. He looked Bella up and down. "Mighty nice rapier you've got there, Lassie. Beautiful matched pair of pistols, too. Seen you shoot yesterday. You're a damn good shot. Mind if I have a look at one of them?"

Bella was reluctant to hand over one of her guns to this stranger, but he seemed harmless enough. Keeping her hand on the butt of one pistol, she handed the other one over for Mac to examine.

He gave a low whistle. "Now there's something you don't see every day, rifled barrels on a pair of pistols. Dueling pistols, English make. Very nice." He handed the gun back to her, and Bella breathed a silent sigh of relief. "Stay put here, Lassie, and I'll be back with some tea for your tum. The galley is one deck below, and the hold below that."

Bella, unfamiliar with nautical terms, was not sure what a "galley" was. She watched Mac descend through another hatch, and then she walked to the nearest cannon, running her hand along the iron barrel. There was surprisingly little rust on its surface considering the guns were exposed to salt spray anytime the ports were open. She examined the weapons inside the arsenal, and they, too, were in top condition. Bella suspected Mac was a man who took great pride in maintaining the weapons. He had looked lovingly on her pistol while examining it.

Mac returned bearing a pewter mug with steam curling up from inside. "Drink this, Lassie. It'll settle you right down, but I warn you, it'll make you a wee bit sleepy." He handed Bella the cup and she sipped the tea. It had an odd, slightly bitter taste, but then she was not a tea drinker and was not sure how tea should taste.

"Speaking of sleep, Lassie, I was thinking you might want to bunk in here." Mac nodded toward the arsenal where his hammock was hung. "Probably the safest place on the ship for you. The door locks from inside or out, and there's only one key." He extended his hand palm up, offering Bella the big iron key.

"Where will you sleep?" she asked.

"Ah, I'll make my bunk down on the crew deck below. I know you bunked with the captain last night ..."

"We did not sleep together."

"I'm not saying you did. It's just that Ned likes his privacy, that and he snores something fierce. This here arsenal can be your own place. Just don't go putting up lace curtains or anything."

Bella laughed. She decided she liked this kind, funny Scotsman. "I gave up lace curtains and girly frills a long time ago." She finished the tea and immediately yawned.

"Go on, Lassie, get some sleep. I'll see to it no one bothers you, but go ahead and lock the door from inside."

Bella was disoriented when she awoke. She had no idea where she was, or whether it was day or night. Then it came back to her, her interaction with Mac and his generosity in giving up his berth for her. A candle lantern with the candle burned almost to a stub hung near the door. Bella looked around at the array of weapons surrounding her, enough to arm a small army, and smiled. Her stomach felt fine, and the rolling of the ship under sail no longer bothered her. She stood, unlocked the door, and went onto the gundeck. Mac was no where around, no one was. She closed and locked the arsenal door and pocketed the key. When she climbed to the main deck, she saw that the sun was low in the west, a fiery red ball just kissing the horizon. She had slept nearly all day and was starving.

Bella was not quite sure what to do, or where to go. She was on a ship in the middle of the sea, with no land in sight. It seemed almost dream-like. She had never imagined herself on a ship, but there she was, and the cool breeze caressing her face and ruffling her hair dispelled any thought that she might be dreaming. She spotted Ned standing on a raised deck above his cabin, so she headed in that direction.

As she passed by a scruffy, bare-chested crewman coiling rope mid-deck, the man unexpectedly grabbed her arm and swung her around. "Give us a kiss, pretty lady."

Bella jerked her arm free and gave the man a hard shove backwards. He fell onto his backside, but quickly scrambled to his feet and pulled out a sheath knife.

"You Bitch! I'll give you another scar to match the one you've already got."

Bella stepped back and drew her rapier. The crewman hesitated, but then two more pirates came at Bella, one on either side, determined to have their way with her. So much for Captain O'Keeffe's promise of protection, Bella thought. She knew he was on the quarterdeck watching the events unfold.

Before any of the three men could grab her again, Bella lunged forward at the man with the knife, and with a flick of her wrist, sliced the razor sharp tip of her sword down the length of the man's forearm. He yowled in pain and dropped the knife as blood gushed from his wound. As quick and agile as a cat, Bella swung around, and with two quick thrusts, inflicted nonfatal wounds on the other two assailants.

Another pirate, an older man with gray muttonchop whiskers and a sparse head of wiry gray hair, was standing next to Ned on the quarterdeck. "Captain, you'd best stop this right now," he said.

"Before she kills half my crew?" Ned laughed. "I wanted to see if she really could handle herself. Looks like she can. I think you've got your work cut out for you." Ned descended to the main deck followed by the other man.

"Enough of this!" Ned bellowed as he approached the scene. By then Bella had sheathed her sword and drawn her pistols, and the three wounded men had staggered away from her. "I told you men this woman was under my protection, not that she seems to need it. This goes for everyone!" he shouted out to the rest of the crewmen gathered around to watch. He turned to Bella. "Put your pistols away. Anyone else tries to molest you, you have my permission to kill them. I know you were holding back." He addressed the three injured crewmen. "After Doc patches you up, you're on half rations and double duty until I say otherwise. You're damn lucky she didn't kill the lot of you. Just so you know, this young woman has probably killed more men than all of you put together, so a word to the wise, leave her alone. Bella Vasquez is part of this crew now, so show some respect."

The man with the muttonchop whiskers introduced himself to Bella. "Barnabus Collier, but everyone calls me Doc." He turned to the wounded men. "You three down to the crew deck so I can sew you up."

"Come with me," Ned said to Bella. "We'll get you something to eat. Slicing and dicing folks is hungry work."

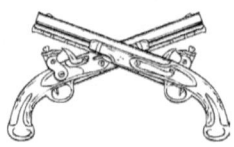

CHAPTER TWENTY-NINE

E veryone on board had either seen or heard about Bella's encounter with the three crewmen. After Ned's second warning, and because of her prowess and reputation, the rest of the crew gave Bella wide berth. She told Ned that Mac had given up his spot in the arsenal, and he agreed it was probably the safest place for her to sleep, both for her and the rest of the crew. He had closely watched her in action, quickly dealing with the three men who assaulted her. Ned had intended to interfere if necessary, but he had never seen anyone as quick and as skilled with a sword as she.

When Bella had been assaulted on that first day aboard, she deliberately held back, fearing that if she killed her attackers, she would either be mobbed by their mates, or thrown off the ship, maybe both. It was a strange new world on board, and she had no idea what rules might apply. She had been on the run for four years, always looking over her shoulder, and she wondered whether this pirate ship would now be home, at least for a while, or was merely a brief stopping place in her life's journey.

Over the next days and weeks she began to develop friendships with Ned and Mac. The man they called Doc also seemed to be one of the crewmen she could trust. After patching up the three men she had wounded, Doc sought Bella out. "That was some mighty fast and fancy sword work," he told her, chuckling. "Remind me not to ever get on your bad side." He told her he was not a real doctor, but had been a medic in the British army. "I do okay digging out pistol balls out of folks, sewing up wounds, setting broken bones and such," he said. "You ever need anything, or got any questions, you can always come to me."

The one crewmember who Bella deliberately avoided was the First Mate, John "The Butcher" Carver. Ever since their first encounter, when Bella outstared him, he tended to avoid her, too. He had been present when Bella displayed her ability defending herself and realized she was not someone to antagonize. Initially he had tried throwing his weight around as First Mate, barking orders at her a few times, but each time she simply stared at him and completely ignored his commands. Ned refused to back up his First Mate, telling him, "Just leave her alone, John." Bella became a unique member of the crew, not only in that she was the only woman on board, but was also the only crewmember with no regularly assigned duties.

It was Ned's hope that Bella would prove her worth if they ever got into a serious fight. Most of the men in his crew were experienced sailors, but only a handful had much actual fighting experience. It seemed strange that a twenty-year-old woman had seen the most action of anyone aboard. Doc had been in the British army, but behind the lines of battle as a medic. Mac had been a gunner on a British frigate, but firing a cannon at another ship from inside a thick, oak bulkhead was far different than shooting at an adversary with pistols at close range, or dueling one-on-one with a sword. Bella had plenty of experience at both. John

"The Butcher" Carver had not earned his moniker because he was ruthless, but because at one time he had actually been a butcher in a meat market in Liverpool. Even Ned, who had served as DeGuillard's First Mate, had only seen limited action running guns during the American War of Independence.

Over the course of the next several weeks, Bella began to learn the ropes of being on a ship at sea. There were a lot of ropes comprising the rigging, and each one had its own particular name, but that was of no concern to her. What she picked up from Ned, Mac, and Doc was the general terminology, learning that the front of the ship was the bow, and the direction toward the front was fore. The rear was the stern, and that direction was called aft. Port was left and starboard right. Ned allowed her to take the wheel from time-to-time to get a feel for steering the ship. He explained to her the use of the compass and sextant to determine the ship's direction and position at sea.

As she became more comfortable in her new environment, Bella explored the other decks, the crew deck where the galley was located, and the hold where supplies were stowed. She spent time with Ned on the quarterdeck above the captain's cabin where the wheel was located, asking dozens of questions about navigation. Ned patiently answered her inquiries, amazed at how quickly she absorbed the information. It became readily apparent that Bella was the most educated member of the crew, thanks to Father Diaz' excellent teaching and her own natural curiosity that had led her to consume most of the books in her father's library.

On occasion she gave fleeting thought to her home, wondering if her father was still alive, and assuming her much younger mother still was. She wondered what her mother, her uncle, and her grandfather would think of her new life at sea. Going home ever again was out of the question, not with a hefty price on her head. She worried that the crew would get word of the reward, and that might be enough of an incentive for a gang of crewmen to try to collect it, they were after all, pirates.

She was, nevertheless, beginning to enjoy being under sail on the blue Caribbean. The breeze on her face, and whipping through her hair was always refreshing. She spent most of her days on deck when the weather was fair, and slept securely locked in the armory at night. After the brief bout of seasickness on her first day aboard, she had gained her sea legs and no longer became queasy no matter how violently the ship rolled, even during heavy tropical storms.

The crew was becoming accustomed to seeing her walk the decks, and after the incident on her first day aboard, left her alone. A few intrepid crewmen tried to woo her with compliments, but she was not interested. The only man aboard she found in any way attractive was Captain Ned O'Keeffe, and it surprised her that he showed absolutely no romantic interest in her.

Bella's first taste of high seas piracy came a few weeks after she joined Ned's crew. The *Queen Maeve* was sailing in the shipping channel between the 600 mile long island of Cuba and the chain of islands known as the Florida Keys. A call came from the crow's nest atop the main mast, "Ship ahoy!"

At the time Bella was standing with Ned on the quarterdeck. Ned pulled out his spyglass to have a look. The ship was a lumbering merchant vessel. "Here, have a look," he said, handing Bella the spyglass, similar to the one Alder had owned, lost with the rest of his possessions when he lost his life. When Bella peered through the glass she noted the all too familiar Spanish flag fluttering in the breeze from the ship's stern.

Ned ordered the helmsman to set a course to intercept the ship. Turning to Bella, he joked, "You do speak some Spanish, don't you?"

"*Si, un poco,*" Bella replied laughing.

"Good. Now it's time for you to earn your keep."

Bella was excited, but also felt a little anxious and unsettled as the *Queen Maeve* closed in on its quarry. Questions about what would soon occur flooded her mind. Was the *Queen Maeve* going to open fire on the

Spanish trade ship? She noted that the starboard gun ports were open and the six cannons on that side had been run out to clear the hull. Would there be fighting? Would the crew of the merchant ship and any passengers aboard be killed, or perhaps held for ransom? It was quite possible that important dignitaries were on board the ship, returning to Spain from duty in Mexico. Bella knew from first-hand experience that during a robbery on land, and presumably also at sea, there was always the possibility of armed resistance.

Ned had descended to the cabin and returned armed with a brace of pistols and a cutlass. A boarding party, led by Carver, was gathered on the main deck. As the *Queen Maeve* came along side the Spanish ship, the *Barcelona*, Ned told Bella to holler for the ship to heave to. She had no idea what that meant, or even how to translate the demand into Spanish, but using her intuition, called out for the ship to furl its sails.

Just then a small contingent of Spanish soldiers, armed with muskets, trooped onto the *Barcelona's* main deck. They must be guards for someone important, Bella thought. She turned to Ned for guidance.

"Tell them to lay down their arms and no one will get hurt. We are only interested in whatever loot is on board."

Bella shouted out Ned's demand. The captain of the military contingent took a look at the six heavy cannons aimed at the *Barcelona* and decided discretion was indeed the better part of valor. To resist with so few men against such overwhelming firepower would be foolish and only end up in death and destruction. Reluctantly, he ordered his men to lay down their arms.

Ropes with grappling hooks attached were thrown from the *Queen Maeve* to the deck of the *Barcelona*. Once the two ships were secured next to each other, planks were laid from rail-to-rail, and the boarding party led by Carver began to cross over.

"Come with me," Ned told Bella. "We'll need a translator."

The Spanish ship's Captain emerged from his cabin, scowling at the army officer who had given in so readily without a fight.

"Tell him we will not harm anyone," Ned told Bella, but before she could translate, the Captain replied in clear English, "Then take what you like and be gone."

Carver's men went to search the ship, while Ned, Bella, and a few men remained on the main deck, keeping an eye on the guards. It was not long before Carver returned, his men carrying strong boxes filled with gold doubloons and silver pesos, a very rich haul. Carver was leading a dignitary, holding the man securely by his upper arm. As soon as Bella saw the man, she froze. He did likewise when he spotted her standing next to Ned.

"*Tio*?" Bella asked in Spanish, shocked to encounter Miguel Navarro, of all people, aboard this ship.

"Isabella? Is that really you? You are with these pirates?"

Bella turned to Ned. "Tell Carver to unhand him. That man is my uncle."

Ned looked at Bella in surprise, but then told Carver to release the man.

"He was hiding in a luxury cabin below," Carver said, still tightly holding Navarro's arm. "We can collect a fat ransom for him."

Bella's hand started to move toward the hilt of her sword, but Ned stayed her hand. "I said release him, John. We aren't taking hostages. We've got more than enough in gold and silver."

Carver reluctantly loosened his grip, and Bella's uncle jerked his arm free. It had been four years since they had seen each other. Her uncle looked older, and tired, but then she had changed, too, no longer a carefree girl of sixteen galloping around her father's hacienda. Bella hesitated a moment, but then moved toward her uncle and embraced him. She took him by the hand and led him away from everyone.

"What has happened to you, goddaughter?" Navarro asked, lightly touching Bella's scar. "You are a wanted outlaw. There is a price on your head. How can that be?"

"It was never what I intended, Uncle. As you know, Father was going to force me into a marriage with that pompous ass, Francisco Moreno, and so I fled. Men tried to assault me, and I killed them. After that I was hunted and I ended up a bandit, and now a pirate. This is not the life I wanted, but it is the life I have."

"Your father is quite ill. You have caused him great embarrassment, great shame."

Bella was quiet a moment. "I do not care. He was never a good father. He never loved me. He wanted a son, not a daughter. The shame should be on him. Is my mother well?"

Miguel shook his head. "I am sorry to tell you, Isabella, but your mother, my dear sister Ana, is dead. She took ill last winter and died."

Bella swallowed hard, and her eyes became misty. That was a blow. Her mother had been much younger than her father, and Bella assumed her mother would live a long lifetime. "You are going back to Spain, Uncle?" Bella wiped her eyes with the sleeve of her blouse.

"Yes. Your grandfather is also dead. His heart gave out. There is nothing left in Mexico for me, so I am returning home to Madrid." Miguel Navarro hesitated a moment. "Come with me, Isabella. I will hire the best lawyers. I know people at the Royal Court. I can get you a pardon from the king. You can start anew."

Bella shook her head. "Thank you, Uncle, but no, I cannot. This is my life now. I have made my bed and I must lie in it. No Spanish gentleman would have me with my scarred face and wicked reputation. My fate is here. Now, I will say goodbye. I wish you a safe journey the rest of the way home, and I am sorry we attacked your ship." Bella again embraced her uncle, and he hugged her back fiercely. He kissed her scarred cheek.

"Take care, Isabella. I am sorry, too, that these bad things have befallen you."

Bella turned away and crossed to the *Queen Maeve*. Ned and the others of the pirate crew followed after her. Carver had already transferred the chests of loot to the *Queen Maeve's* hold. The two ships parted, and Bella stood at the aft rail watching the *Barcelona* sail away. Ned came and stood at her side.

"You were close to your uncle?"

"Yes, he is my godfather. He told me my mother and grandfather have passed away. My father is gravely ill. There is no reason for me to ever return home, even if I could, even if there was no price on my head." She turned her head and looked up at Red Ned. "I will stay aboard your ship, and serve you, my Captain."

Ned nodded. He hesitated a moment, and then clasped her hand in his, glad to have her as a permanent part of the crew They stood together at the rear of the quarterdeck watching the *Barcelona's* sails dip behind the horizon.

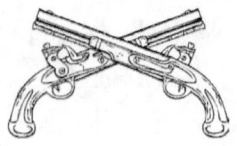

EPILOG

For the next ten years the *Queen Maeve* was a scourge to shipping in the Caribbean and the near Atlantic. Unlike other pirates, Captain Ned O'Keeffe was not bloodthirsty. He tried to avoid fighting whenever possible, but at times sea battles became inevitable. Warships of the major seafaring nations, England, Spain, France, and Holland prowled the seas, trying to root out pirates and guarding convoys of merchant vessels. Piracy became a much more dangerous game. The *Queen Maeve* was no match for much larger and more heavily armed ships-of-the-line. In addition to warships of the major seafaring powers, Ned also had to be concerned about merchant ships that often mounted cannons of their own and enlisted mercenaries to guard precious cargo. Ned could never be sure whether he would be in for a fight when attacking a lumbering merchantman.

Whenever a fight ensued, Bella found herself right in the thick of it. Her deadly prowess with pistols and sword made her a fierce adversary and an invaluable asset to Ned's crew. As her notoriety as a pirate spread, the price on her head was eventually raised to 500 pieces of gold.

Late in the fall of 1795 the *Queen Maeve* set sail for the west coast of Ireland. Ned had heard from an acquaintance, another sea captain, that there was a man in Ned's home town of Galway who might have a job for a man with a good fast ship. The news was short on details, but Ned thought it might be a chance to go legitimate. Piracy was getting too risky. Ned had not been home in twelve years. He wanted to check in on his spinster sister, Mary, who was raising Ned's daughter, Skelly O'Keeffe. He had not seen his daughter even once in those twelve years, not since the girl was two.

It was a cold and rough crossing of the North Atlantic at that time of year. The *Queen Maeve* dropped anchor in a sheltered bay a little north of Galway, and Ned rowed to shore in a small lifeboat. Carver took a party ashore in the ship's longboat to procure supplies. Bella chose to remain on board. She had gone ashore numerous times when the ship stopped for supplies, or anchored off one or another of the many islands dotting the Caribbean. Going ashore always seemed to lead to trouble. Her distinguishing scar made her a target for anyone wanting to collect the hefty reward for her capture. She always managed to escape, and at times did so without leaving bodies in her wake. She had no idea whether her notoriety had spread as far as Ireland, but decided not to take any chances by going ashore.

Ned was gone for several days, and when he returned to the ship he was not alone. A young "lad" of around fourteen or so accompanied him. Ned introduced the "boy" to the crew as his nephew, Skelly, and most of the crew was fooled by the "boy's" shortened hair and male clothing—pants, shirt, vest and cap—but Bella immediately realized that Ned's "nephew" was actually a girl. She watched as Ned led the girl aft, toward his cabin. The girl had bright red hair, the same shade as Ned's. I guess I had better go and see what this is all about, Bella told herself. She stood up from the crate where she had been sitting, oiling her pistols, and followed Ned and the girl to the captain's cabin. Little did she know that her pending interaction with the red-haired girl would soon lead to adventures of a completely different kind.

The End

You can read more of Isabella Vasquez' story in:
A Pirate's Daughter, and in *Captain Skelly O'Keefe; Around the Horn*.
Both books are available from Amazon.

www.ingramcontent.com/pod-product-compliance
Lightning Source LLC
Chambersburg PA
CBHW050937120626
46552CB00001B/247